One

It was the month of October, Josephine had  restaurant and the evening had gone well. Ho her mind that was troubling her. The air was w The atmosphere was peaceful, and she looked up towards. She was overwhelmed by the majesty of such great creativity.

As she walked along the path that led to her home, she heard the sudden slam of a nearby door; a young girl came running out of one of the houses. Her feet were bare, as she held her shoes in her hand, she was sobbing. Josephine wanted to help but the girl disappeared in a flash. What could have happened to of upset her? It put Josephine's troubles into perspective.

Josephine finally reached the security gate by the side of her house. She inserted the key in the lock, for some reason the gate was stuck. She tried again, in a slight panic at the thought of being unable to get into her home after midnight. The darkness added to her confusion. She turned the key once again, and this time the gate opened. Such was Josephine's state of mind that she wondered momentarily whether she would be able to get into her home. As the front door opened at the first time of trying, she told herself that she had been watching too many horror films. Before very long, she was relaxing in front of the television with a cup of hot chocolate.

Dinner at Mickey's restaurant had been to celebrate that Samantha, one of Josephine's work colleagues, was getting married in December. It was an all-girl affair. Josephine loved Italian cuisine, the food and the wine was wonderful. The women had been in great spirits so there was much laughter as they related of great tales of the past. Josephine was pleased that they were all so happy to talk about themselves that she did not need to say very much.

Samantha was a good looking woman, tall and slim with long blond silky hair, whereas Cathy and Barbara were less striking. They had a distinct individuality and strength of character. Their hair was always well groomed and their make-up beautifully applied, they also knew how to dress. The girls were noted for their well- tailored suits and outfits' although they had such a similar way of dressing that it sometimes seemed to Josephine that they must compare notes.

Josephine felt at a slight disadvantage working with these women. She did not have Samantha's looks, or the sophistication and intellectual capacity of Cathy and Barbara. At least that was how she saw things, but she found it quite challenging to work with them. The truth was that they were living the sort of lives that she wanted to live yet it seemed to her that their prospects, both in personal and in business terms, were better than hers.

Physically, Josephine did not regard herself as very attractive. In fact, quite the opposite. When she looked in the mirror, she saw a woman of five foot five, with short shoulder- length brown hair, blue eyes and a standard face, but without much expression. Her boyfriend called her beautiful. For him, her personality shone through her face and made her big blue eyes sparkle. That was one of the things that attracted him to her in the first place. She would not give herself credit. She thought however her face only glowed on occasions, and never when she was overworked, which was nearly always, or when she was emotionally withdrawn. Which was really when things were not going well at home, like now, or when she was unhappy because she had broken her diet by eating a cream bun or a chocolate bar, which happened nearly every week? She was not fat, but she did need to watch what she ate to keep her average figure average.

The two other women at dinner were Jackie and Simone. Confident, attractive and laid back about everything, Jackie was half- Ghanaian and half- Welsh and just naturally beautiful. Simone, skinny and radiant, was half- Chinese and half- English. [They were never without boyfriends, whereas Cathy and Barbara were always fighting over men they liked].

Josephine was never uncomfortable with these friends but she was particularly happy with Samantha. There was one particular woman in the office that she did find difficult to cope with. A newly- wed when she took the job, she was pregnant five months later. This was great news and Josephine was excited for her. However by the fourth month of the pregnancy, the woman began to look exceptionally radiant and managed to remain stylish and attractive despite her slightly bulging stomach. In fact the baby shone through her, making her more beautiful than she had ever been.

Surprisingly, this created a moment of pain for Josephine, who wanted what her colleague had. Josephine was a manageress and had the status and the extra salary, but was jealous of the woman's pregnancy.

Unfortunately, that was something her boyfriend Paul was totally opposed to. He wanted to remain a bachelor and to stay in the fast lane, free of children and expensive responsibilities. He was an exciting person to be associated with but was not ready to slow down and think sensibly about his future. At times he was very selfish and boyishly childlike, despite the fact that he was aged thirty-seven. Josephine herself was only three years younger and was worried about still being single, but whenever she talked to Paul about settling down and starting a family, he was always ready with an excuse.

There was a young man called Leonard who worked in the same office. Although only twenty, he looked quite mature. In fact, he was an inch shorter than Josephine but was handsome, with stylish brown hair. His suits always looked as though they had just come from the dry cleaners. He made a point of talking to Josephine about his girlfriend Sally, whenever problems arose in their relationship, which was most of the time. She found it really quite sweet listening, especially when his problems seemed like nothing compared to hers. The couple had been dating for four years since Sally was only fourteen, and Leonard would talk solemnly about his childhood sweetheart and all their ups and downs, and asked Josephine for advice. She did not offer much because she did not feel particularly qualified to do so.

She felt very melancholy when Samantha got married during the second week in December, and was not in the best of moods when she attended the office Christmas party. She had invited Paul but he had other arrangements of his own. Leonard was also upset because his girlfriend couldn't make it. He clung to Josephine, who drank a little too much. He made sure that her glass was always full. After a time, they left the premises to get some fresh air. Josephine really enjoyed being with him. He seemed a welcome escape from the dreary realism of her personal life. Before she knew it, their hands had clasped and he bought her close to him. She felt his warm breath on her face. She was tempted to kiss him. She was quite surprised at his response, and that moment was the most passionate moment she had had in months.

Back at the office on Monday she regretted everything that had taken place. In a sense she was Leonard's immediate boss and was worried that he might be seen as her toy boy. Josephine prayed that he wouldn't say anything to anyone else, but paranoia set in every time she saw him talking to a male colleague, especially when they seemed to be sharing a joke. It felt as though everyone in the office was watching her. The atmosphere around her seemed to tell its own great tale, and this state of affairs continued for several weeks. She sensed a loss of respect from some of her fellow workers.

She was disappointed in Leonard, but continued to talk to him in a professional manner. This became more difficult when she suspected that she was not wrong in thinking that he had talked about her to his colleagues.

When returning to the office one afternoon after lunch, she noticed Leonard and some friends gathered together. They obviously did not know she was present. She stood by a filing cabinet in a corner and listened to their conversation. She could hardly believe her ears. A casual kiss had now been blown up into a full-scale affair, but then she remembered that the kiss didn't really feel casual and his touch felt so responsive. Leonard was saying that a serious relationship existed between them but they did not want to go public with it, entirely for professional reasons.

'She is head over heels in love with me, and every night she begs me to leave my girlfriend so she can have me all to herself, Leonard said.

'No!' said Nigel.

'Oh yes, she really wants to leave her boyfriend but is scared of being alone.' said Leonard.

'She's not brilliantly attractive. She's probably scared of not getting anyone else,' said another colleague.

'Yes, she really wants me to move in with her after she gets rid of her boyfriend,' Leonard added.

'Who is he?' asked Nigel.

'Some sales manager. Who works in an office in the West End.'

'Then why would she want to go out with you if she's got such a high-powered boyfriend?' asked another colleague.

This was an awkward question and Leonard considered for a moment before replying.

'I don't know. Maybe he's interested in a proper dolly bird and is giving her the big heave-ho. But anyway all I know is that she's a good opportunity to fulfil my ambition.'

'Ambition! What ambition?' asked Nigel

'To get her job, become a manager. A man should run this office, not a woman!'

'Yes, but you're so young and inexperienced.'

'Yeah, well she didn't seem to think so.'

Josephine felt quite sick.

'Anyway, how are you going to do it?' asked Nigel

'By blackmail!'

'Yes, see these pictures? Look closely. I had a friend take them when she was drunk at the party and then threw herself at me outside.'

The whole incident had been planned in advance, Josephine realised. There were obviously several photographs and Leonard had only chosen to get close to her to set up this sordid scenario. What was worse was that he had waited until he could pretend that a real relationship had developed between them.

'So what are you going to do with the photographs?' asked Nigel.

'I'll talk to Josephine about my career prospects, and if she's not prepared to help me, I'll show them to her.'

'Man, you've got a wicked streak in you, but won't you endanger your job by doing this?' asked Lee.

'No, just watch me, I've thought everything through.'

Josephine could hardly believe that an innocent kiss could result in blackmail' or that she had befriended a young man who was prepared to go to such lengths to take her job. She felt very insecure and realised that she was shaking, but some inner strength came to her aid. There was a side to her character that she had never been called upon to use.

The deepest, blackest thoughts crossed her mind. Would she take revenge? Her mother had told her about her own difficulties. Which had required great strength to overcome. And she had hoped that her daughter would find the same strength of character if she were ever faced with similar problems. Josephine did not understand what her mother was trying to teach her, but she knew that Leonard had to be stopped and somehow she would find a way to remove this man from the office and out of her life.

Two

Yet what could she do and how could she handle the situation? At first, when she heard Leonard talking, she was overcome with emotion and had to hold onto the other side of the door and count to twenty in order to calm down. The pain that assailed her was extraordinary. Her mind raced around, and she swallowed, as a lump seemed to form in her throat. Fresh air was what she needed.

As she stood there in disbelief, the situation did not seem real. But it was real, although she was in utter confusion. She slowly walked out of the building, looking down at her nails, observing them to see if they needed to be manicured.

'Nail varnish' she thought, 'yes that reminds me, I need more nail varnish.' Why on earth was she thinking about such a triviality when she should have been planning how to deal with Leonard? She knew that her mind was trying to escape the truth and she would have to get her act together and deal with the problem.

Perhaps she should talk to Leonard and persuade him to tell his colleagues that he had made the whole thing up, or at least exaggerated. That would be a civilised way of approaching the situation. She was not a vindictive person, and had never been in a situation where she felt that she needed to take revenge. They say that revenge is sweet, but she did not really think so. However, she was now dealing with a twenty year old man who probably did not even know his own mind, but who could perhaps ruin her career. Something she had worked very hard at to achieve her present situation. But what really disgusted her was that Leonard had set the whole thing up and arranged to have pictures taken of something that was quite innocent, but could be interpreted as something more serious. She thought of talking to her boss but was worried that he might not believe her.

Josephine was the only female manager in the company, and had succeeded to this position with much difficulty. And was aware of certain sexiest comments from the other managers, but did not let them bother her. She just got on with her job, which she did very well. And was uncertain how much support she could expect from her senior colleagues. Everything she had worked for might be at risk.

Her fear began to subside when she found herself at last able to make certain decisions. First she would telephone the receptionist to inform her that that she was taking a long lunch break.

Then she would go to the gym for a quick workout followed by a sauna and a shower. She had become a member because she found that attending the gym helped her to create a more positive attitude when she was feeling depressed. A good workout gave her a better mental outlook and improved her appearance. She had been very unhappy about Paul, he did not seem to love her enough to enable her to fulfil her dream of marriage and a family life. She hoped that it might help if she herself felt able to approach life more positively. To anyone listening to Leonard in the office, she must have sounded pathetic, which meant that she probably looked pathetic, She might not be the most attractive person in the world but she could make the most of her good points. If she looked and felt good, it would give her strength to face her problems.

The work-out did wonders for her, and as Josephine stood looking at herself in the mirror, she really began to like what she saw, and what she was thinking. The fear she felt had disappeared, as sudden warmth filled her body. She felt decisive. No way would she allow Leonard to ambush her into thinking that he could take her job through blackmail. Things were going to change at the office, but not at Leonard's dictation. She would also take steps to improve her personal life.

Three

It was amazing the sudden strength she now felt. Having decided to change both her inner and outer self, she was determined to do so quickly. She would work out regularly and completely change her diet to get her physique back into shape. She hoped that within two weeks there would be a complete change.

After leaving the gym she felt an extreme zest for life. Instead of going back to the office, she walked into the hairdresser and had her hair completely re-styled by having it layered in order to create more body and character. She also decided to dye it chestnut brown, emphasizing her blue eyes. All she needed now was some make-up and luckily the beautician had just come back from lunch and was able to apply a professional finishing touch to her appearance.

Josephine could not believe that what she was looking at was her own image. She could not have been more pleased with the transformation. There was something different about her, a sort of radiance. After leaving the salon, she walked briskly with a bounce in every step back to the office.

As soon as she walked through the doors everyone from the receptionist and the cleaner to her work colleagues stopped what they were doing. They could not believe the sudden change in Josephine's appearance, or the unusual way in which she addressed them.

'Hi guys.' She said confidently.

Everyone was watching her. She smiled as she sorted out the messages that had been left on her desk. She felt Leonard's eyes piercing through her, as he wondered why she had decided today of all days to change her appearance so drastically and why she was so happy. He assumed that she had not heard his earlier conversation because he knew that would have broken her. Leonard knew what women were like and that she would have cried, and gone into a deep depression and then start feasting on chocolate bars and crisps. He thought he knew women inside out. In fact, it was part of his plan that Josephine would overhear some of his conversation in order to depress her.

'Hi, Josephine,' he eventually called out. 'I must say, you're looking lovelier than ever.'

Josephine had pretended that she had not heard him but immediately answered another colleague who questioned her.

Leonard felt embarrassed and hurt by this. She had not even raised her head when he spoke to her. He blushed when he saw one of his male colleagues smirking at him.

Josephine's revenge was already starting to work.

Four

Over the weekend, Josephine continued to indulge herself, trying further to improve her appearance, and planning to be friendlier to people in the office. Her professional wardrobe consisted of neutral colours such as navy blue, black and white, but now she decided to wear some fiery colours, including red, orange and yellow. When she arrived in the office on Monday morning with a bounce in her step and an enormous smile on her face, again there was complete silence.

Many of the men had been suffering from hangovers since Saturday evening and were unused to receiving shocks first thing in the Monday morning. The women were too surprised to react instantly because it was unknown for Josephine to walk into the office looking fabulous and happy at any time. They were puzzled why this sudden change had taken place and when they smelt the subtle scent of her expensive perfume; they could hardly take their eyes off her.

To Josephine's annoyance, some people assumed that her transformation was due to her new relationship with Leonard, of course did nothing to discourage such speculation.

'So what's happening between you and Josephine?' Colin asked him. 'I can't believe how much she's changed.'

Leonard blushed and lowered his head, for once somewhat lost for words.

'Oh you know, we had the usual Saturday night on the town, and then back to her flat for a coffee, and the rest I'll leave to your imagination.'

He was pleased with the sentence that had suddenly evolved. The fact that there was no truth in it did not worry him until his friend Jack came into the office, sat down at his desk and yelled over to him, so that everyone could hear.

'We had a great evening on Saturday night, didn't we?'

Leonard nodded as imperceptibly as possible but Matthew took the point up.

'I thought you spent the evening with Josephine, 'he said.

'I did, but then I decided to meet up with Jack and go to a night-club.'

'Oh,' said Matthew, looking very confused.

No one was more confused, however, than Leonard. A lump began to fill in his throat because he could not understand what was going on in Josephine's mind. He began to view her differently. Everything about her began to entice him into really wanting to be with her. Even her personality seemed to be changing and her new look totally captivated him. He had treated her as a figure of fun and humiliated her but amazingly, and almost instantly, he found himself falling in love with her.

He knew he would have to control his feelings before he made a fool of himself in front of his friends, but this was not easy. The one thing that really hurt him at that moment Josephine was completely ignoring him just when he really wanted her to notice him.

The questions still continued and he was having more and more difficulty in dealing with them.

One of them was very direct. 'When you went back to jo's flat, where was the boyfriend?'

'Oh, he was on a business trip,' Leonard replied after much hesitation.

For once he was telling the truth because Paul was indeed away on a business trip. From Josephine's point of view there had been too many of these business trips lately. In fact, she had been wondering whether Paul was having an affair. She had turned a blind eye to many situations that confirmed the possibility. He sometimes arrived home as if he had been on holiday, with flushed cheeks and a sort of radiance, which made her suspicious. Among all the lies that Leonard had spoken about her, one thing he said might have been true. Was she clinging onto Paul because she was scared of being alone and unable to get another partner? She had become so used to Paul after five years together she was quite scared of leaving him and diving into another relationship, uncertain of the outcome.

It wasn't only the shock of Leonard's betrayal, and the need to perhaps dump Paul and seek other male company that made her decide to make a conscious change in her appearance and attitude, to make the very best of herself and allow her qualities to be fully displayed in order to create a more positive and confident person.

She needed to deal both with Paul and Leonard from a position of strength, and was determined to make the best of herself and enjoy life to the full.

Five

Back at home she finally made the irrevocable decision, one that should have been made a long time ago. It was only now that she saw that Paul's interest in her was entirely selfish, there was no future in it. The chances were that it would turn out bleak and miserable. It was not only a painful decision to make, but a necessary.

Suddenly it felt strange to find an inner force to enable her to take charge of the situation and to make important changes in her life. She thought she knew herself well she was becoming aware that there was more of a decisive side to her personality. It was an exciting discovery, but at the same time a scary one because she had no idea of what might be in store for her. She was trying to change her life for the better but knew that she was risking her security in the process.

As she stood looking at some of the photographs of herself and Paul alongside a married couple with a baby on a beach in Portugal, she could hardly believe that three years had passed since that particular holiday. They had been so happy then, so much in love. She just could not understand what had gone wrong. Or maybe she did, but did not want to acknowledge the reason. She knew subconsciously as the selfish side of Paul's personality slowly revealed itself, her attitude towards him changed. His behaviour gradually began to eat away at their relationship.

She was seized by a wave of emotion and started to sob as she thought how better things could have been if she had handled them differently. Then again maybe it was better that they had not married and had children because of the future would have been more painful. She sighed and sat down on the side of the arm chair as she wiped away her tears. The pain she was experiencing slowly subsided as she began to think how lucky she was still to have another chance of finding happiness.

She would make a clean break with Paul and at the same time do all that was necessary at work to protect herself from Leonard and save her career.

She felt a strong sense of loneliness as she gathered all the pictures she could find of herself and Paul and put them in a plastic bag. Next, she went into the bathroom and placed all Paul's toiletries into another bag. She took particular pleasure in throwing in the ponytail hair extension, which he liked to wear to impress some of his young clients, [so he said, or was it the women?]. She could not help laughing when she remembered the occasion when he had worn it at the disco and it revealed a mind of its own by falling on the floor while he was doing his John Travolta act in front of a large crowd. Her memory of the ensuing uproar made it easier for her to empty his clothes out of the wardrobe and the chest of drawers. Out of the respect for the amount the clothes had cost. She placed them not in bags but in suitcases, which she left in the corner in the room.

She did not know how Paul was going to react, but having determined to create a decent life for herself; she wanted her decision to be final. He would probably fight and try to persuade her to take him back, but she was at peace with her decision, and knew she was doing the right thing.

Paul came home two days later.

'Hi, Josie, I'm here,' he called out. 'Did you miss me?'

She remained silent.

'I missed you,' he said as he came through the door. 'So, what have you been up to?'

'Oh this and that,' was all she could manage to mutter.

'That sounds exciting' he said.

He went straight into the bathroom without even kissing her on the cheek.

'Josie, have you seen my brown towel?'

'yes'

'Well, where is it?'

'It should be in one of the suitcases.'

'Suitcase? What are you talking about?

'Didn't you notice anything when you walked into the bedroom?'

'Yes,' he said slowly, 'my brown towel is missing.'

'Didn't you notice anything else?'

Paul went back into the bathroom. It was only then that he realised that all his things had gone.

'Jo what's going on, have we had a burglary?' He asked. He obviously he did not know what to make of the situation.

Josephine did not trust herself to speak. It was much better to let him find out for himself.

He went back into the bedroom and his voice became serious.

'What are the suitcases doing here?' he demanded.

'Guess,' was all she said.

Josephine, what are you playing at? I come home from a business trip...'

'Really' she interrupted in a sarcastic tone.

'Yes, I come home from a business trip and find that you've packed up all my belongings. It's as though you're saying you don't want me to live with you anymore.'

'Correct, you've got it in one. Thanks'.

'Thanks for what?'

'Thanks for saving me from having to tell you what you've just said.'

There was silence as Paul tried to make sense of what he was hearing. He looked at her carefully for the first time since he had come home.

'Josephine, do you know what you're saying? Good grief, what have you done to yourself? You look so different. What have you done to your eyes?

They're piercing blue!

She had bought herself a new pair of contact lenses.

'What have you done to your hair?'

'I've had it re-styled.

'And what have you done to your face? You look so much fresher. You look quite beautiful, do you know that?'

'Thank you, and it's all because of this one decision I made, a few days ago.'

'And what was that?'

'To get rid of you.'

If that sounded brutal it had to be said. It left Paul feeling very confused. 'You don't know what you're saying, darling.'

'Oh yes I do,' she said bluntly'

'But what, Why this sudden change? I thought we were happy.'

'Maybe you were, living your double life, but I definitely wasn't.'

'What do you mean a double life?

This was very uncomfortable for Paul, who stared at the floor, and began to rub his neck and slowly loosen his tie.

'You really thought I didn't know, didn't you?'

'Know about what?'

'About your new female friend, what's her name?'

She had no proof but was convinced she was right. Her bombshell had the desired affect

'Lorna,' he said in high confusion. 'I mean, how did you... what are you talking about, Josephine?

'OK, the game's up. So her name's Lorna. Yes, I've known there was someone for a while.'

'How did you?'

'Because of your behaviour. I could sense it in everything you did. It was obvious that you were messing around.'

He was too astonished to respond.

'Come on, Paul,' she said' 'it's ok, we're not married, even though I thought we were committed to each other. That was the main reason we decided to live together, but obviously you had your own ideas.'

'Please Josephine.'

'Why don't you just admit it and realise that our relationship is over? I had great plans for our future, but they depended on us both having a mature outlook on life. You've got alot of growing up to do, Paul. Let's just call it a day.'

As soon as she threw him out, although the mortgage on the flat was in joint names, Paul tried to revive the relationship by buying her expensive flowers and chocolates, which she could have done without. A dress and perfume would be better; he even gave her a sports car. She expected everything on the principal that it was about time he started treating her like a lady. He owed her some respect and she saw no reason not to accompany him to the theatre when he provided tickets, although she knew it was deceitful to take the gifts when she had no intention to resuming the relationship.

She laughed to herself when Paul got his mum's, sister and brother to ring her up and tell her how much he loved her and that he wanted her to become part of his family. The word 'marriage' was suddenly heard for the first time. This certainly made her stop and think. It would have been welcomed almost any time in the last five years, but now she remembered how deceitful he could be in order to get what he wanted, so she did not encourage him.

She came home one evening to find a letter from him, telling her how much he loved her and asking her to give him another chance. He offered to put the flat in her name to provide security for herself and their future family. She considered this for some time and decided it was too good an opportunity to miss, although it meant living with a man she no longer trusted. After much thought, she agreed to the arrangement and the legal formalities were completed in just over a month.

They were back together again but things were not the same. Paul was more attentive then before but Josephine no longer had the same interest and she even began to hope that he would not mention the 'M'- word. A year ago she would have jumped at the chance of starting a family, but now she knew Paul would not be the father of her children.

She knew in her heart that this arrangement could not continue for long. Even if Paul thought she had tricked him into surrendering his share of the flat, she must get out of this unsatisfactory situation.

Fate came to her aid, she found out by chance that, although she might have been his first lady, he was still seeing Lorna. This confirmed how deceitful he could be.

For the second and last time, she packed his bags and threw him out.

Six

It felt strange living in a flat all by herself. She decided to repaint the white walls in a shade of pale gold as a token of independence, but that was all she changed.

Everything else remained exactly as before. The brown leather sofa and matching armchairs were extremely comfortable. The cream carpet and shaggy rug was still fairly new and in good condition.

She began to enjoy her job more than ever before. It was amazing how much better she was being treated, all because she had decided to change her appearance. The men particular had more time for her and more respect.

She had had little time recently to worry about Leonard and his plans to take her job. Perhaps the talk of blackmail had been no more than bravado to impress his mail colleagues. Leonard no longer seemed a threat. In fact he was bending over backwards to get her attention. He had obviously taken a leaf out of her own book by trying to better his appearance. He had a smart new haircut and bought two expensive suits and some designer ties.

Josephine assumed rightly that the ties were meant for her eyes, but she did not give Leonard the attention he wanted. It would serve him right if he made a fool of himself in front of his colleagues. And she still wanted to punish him, for the disgraceful way he had treated her. In some ways she was grateful that he had put her in a predicament; it had revealed to her inner strength that she did not realise she possessed. Josephine had found the courage to turn adversity into something positive. The threat of her security also made her see that her personal life was a shame. Once Leonard had put doubts in her mind about her relationship with Paul, she was never able to look at Paul in the same light. To that extent she was grateful to Leonard. She could see now that Paul was dragging her down, not only affecting her personal life but also her work. He had never encouraged her to make the best of herself. Having got rid of him, she felt at last her life was in good order and ready for the next step forward.

On many occasions she would walk into the office to find a red rose on her desk, with a letter in a sealed envelope bearing the words, Guess Who?' Once she received a bouquet of flowers, with the wording, I really like your new look.' One day there was even a gold pen with the inscription 'To Josephine', this had to be Leonard trying to apologise, but Josephine suspected from the frequency and value of the gifts, that he was trying to say more. She was determined however to play it cool and did not give him any undue attention. If Josephine were honest with herself, she would have to admit that she did think Leonard rather attractive, but of course he had completely let her down by his unacceptable behaviour. And she only spoke to him when necessary and for most of the time completely ignored him.

She could not be absolutely certain that it was Leonard who was her secret admirer but was given the opportunity to find out for certain when she received the invitation to dinner on Friday night at a particular Italian restaurant in the West End. She found it difficult to resist Italian food, but just in case it was not Leonard who invited her, she decided to ask Cathy and Barbara to accompany her. They were to stay in the background, for which reason it was better to have a table in the rear of the restaurant. Even if it were Leonard, it would be sensible to have witnesses in case the invitation was a setup.

That particular Friday, Leonard seemed continually to be looking at her, hoping to catch her attention, but she refused to satisfy his curiosity. Assuming it was him who had invited her out, she let him wonder whether she would turn up. This gave her a great deal of contentment, because it was good to think that she had her life in order, her job under control and that she no longer felt threatened.

She did a small amount of weekend shopping at a local supermarket before returning home after work. She knew exactly what she was going to wear. Anticipating that her social life would resume after Paul's departure, she had bought herself two brand new dresses, one a startling red and the other a black –off-the-shoulder number. She decided to be a scarlet lady for this evening. The red dress had thin shoulder straps and she also bought a red laced shawl to cover her shoulders. She wore high- heeled gold sandals and carried a small gold handbag.

When she walked into the restaurant, she produced the invitation, with the table number written on it. Cathy and Barbara walked in and were shown to their table. They were soon absorbed in conversation. Josephine could see from the expression on their faces that they were bowled over by her outfit. They had been used to a more conservative Josephine, perhaps in a well- tailored suit in a neutral colour.

'Good on you girl,' thought Cathy to herself as she waved to Josephine, who was wearing a glossy red lipstick. The effect was stunning.

At that very moment, Josephine's secret admirer came in through the door. Any doubts she may have had were removed. It was indeed Leonard.

'Josephine,' he said as soon as the waiter had shown him to the table, 'You look great'.

'Thank you, Leonard, so it is you'.

'Yes, of course, who did you think it was?

'I thought it was you but I wasn't sure you'd have the nerve after the way you behaved.'

'Josephine, you look absolutely beautiful, what on earth have you been doing to yourself?'

She did not want to make things too easy for him.

I'm the same person I've always been,' she said holding her head up in the air.

'How's Sally?' she continued after a pause.

'Oh, she's fine,' he said, turning away quickly to change the subject. Would you like some wine?

The arrival of the wine seemed to break the ice and they both started to relax and enjoy the evening. The meal was delicious and Josephine found that she was happy to being Leonards Company. She was pleased to linger over coffee and mints. There was no sign of anyone taking photographs and she was beginning to think that Leonard's interest in her was now genuine.

'Shall I take you home now?' he suddenly asked. It was after eleven.

'I'll manage on my own, thank you. I really do appreciate the evening, Leonard, but we can call it a day for now?

'If that's what you want, but how will you get home?'

'I've ordered a cab for 11.15'.

Leonard looked at his watch.

'Do you want me to wait until it arrives? It will be here in ten minutes'.

'No, don't worry, I'll be fine. I'll see you on Monday.'

Leonard had hoped that she might have wanted to see him the following evening, and as he drove home he was annoyed with himself for not suggesting another date.

Once he was out of sight, Cathy and Barbara joined Josephine.

'I thought he would never leave 'Barbara said. 'You two sure seemed to be enjoying yourselves.'

Josephine said nothing and was pleased when the taxi arrived before she needed to comment. Her friends accompanied her back to her house were they stayed overnight.

Seven

While she had been living with Paul, she would never have thought of having her friend stay with her, even when he was away on business. It gave her extreme excitement having Cathy and Barbara in the flat. She was tired when she got home but they stayed up .watching comedy videos, for a while.

'So what are you doing tomorrow evening?' Cathy suddenly asked. It was usually Cathy who asked the leading questions, which was why Josephine thought of her friends as Cathy and Barbara rather than Barbara and Cathy.

'Tomorrow evening?' for Josephine' one night of entertainment was enough to think about.

'Yes tomorrow. Come on, girl, you're a free woman now. It's time for you to start enjoying yourself.'

'What about a club?' Barbara suggested.

'That would be brilliant. I'd love to go nightclubbing up West', said Cathy

Josephine was doubtful. 'Nightclubbing?' she said

'Yes what's wrong with that?'

'It's just that I haven't been to a night club for ages.'

She was thankful at least that her friends did not ask her if she had made another date with Leonard. She wanted to feel liberated, but in her own good time, and things were beginning to happen rather too quickly for her.

They woke up late on Saturday morning. Cathy and Barbara left after midday, and arranged to return by eight 0clock that evening. Josephine spent the day tidying up and shopping, and then cooked some roast chicken so that there was food for the girls if they wanted something to eat either before or after their evening out, as It only needed warming up. In fact they tucked into it with gusto after a very pleasant evening on the town. Josephine wondered why she had any doubts about going out two nights in a row.

On Monday morning she arrived at the office bright and early. Within five minutes of being there, Leonard walked through the door.

She greeted him instantly. 'Hi, Leonard, how are you?'

I'm fine thanks, Josephine, 'he replied. 'It was great to see you Friday evening. You caused quite a stir in your wonderful red dress. Everyone was admiring you.'

'Really?' she tried to sound surprised.' I didn't notice.'

'You know what I was hoping?

She took a deep breath.   ' what?' she said, knowing what was coming and not totally sure that she wanted to hear it.

'I would like us to get it together. I really like you, Josephine, and I would like to take you out, even start dating you.'

'The dating is out of the question, Leonard!'

'Why?' The sharpness of her response had startled him.

'She thought that it was obvious after all the...'

She stopped herself in mid- sentence. He did not know that she had overheard the boastful conversation with his colleagues when he had even spoken about blackmail. Something told her to stay quiet. The pain she had suffered had given her an inner strength and amazingly within such a short span of time she was able to cope.

She made decision there and then that she would not allow Leonard's past misbehaviour get the better of her.

'All right,' she now said. 'I will go out with you, and we'll see how it goes.'

He was totally taken aback by the change in her attitude, but his pleasure was obvious.

'Great,' 'what about Saturday, would that be OK?'

'Let's make it Friday evening again.'

She had enjoyed herself so much with Cathy and Barbara that she had decided to make Saturday evenings a girl's night out. This week they were planning to go to the pictures in Leicester Square and then to Chinatown for a meal. Josephine was keen on Chinese food, but agreed because Cathy and Barbara loved it so much.

The week went well. Leonard's professional conduct was impeccable.

Now that he was taking her out, he no longer sought any special attention from her in the office. She had one or two lingering doubts about going out with him again, but she felt so under control that she did not care what he told his work mates. She had heard the worst and nothing he could say would hurt her in the future.

Leonard had obviously learnt a thing or two about his earlier misconduct and he was beginning to keep his private life to himself. Or was this just a game?

Eight

As Josephine and Leonard began to date, at first she felt tense and stressed with the situation and even breathless at times, when her heart began to race. She learnt to take deep breaths and relax, and suddenly she would find herself under control once again. She was a straight forward person with straight forward ideas, but was worried that she might be playing a dangerous game. Leonard was primarily concerned with himself and she could not be certain that there was any future in their relationship, even if she wanted there to be. She did not want to ask him any questions; it was early days anyway. The one thing that was important to her was not to lose control of the situation, so she was inclined to hold back even if it made her feel a bit hypocritical because she found him attractive.

As they grew to know each other better, she was able to relax more and it was not long before she began to feel positively happy, almost for the first time in her life.

Leonard had matured since the first time they had gone out. He was more of a gentleman, opening doors for her and helping her with her chair. Other people seemed to respect her more now that she was taking greater pride in her appearance.

Within six months of dating, she felt sufficiently secure about Leonard. By then she was in any case pregnant. Far from being a threat to her at work, he was extremely supportive. She in turn gave him all the encouragement she could, and it was not long before he was appointed the youngest supervisor in the office. His association with her had given him a sort of maturity which was recognised by his work colleagues, and this in turn increased in confidence.

Josephine was happy within herself, especially with the pregnancy. It had not been planned but she was pleased that she had made herself physically vulnerable so that such a miracle could occur. Leonard had been shocked at first, then went through a phase thinking that he was some sort of god because he had planted an embryo inside of her. She was a bit annoyed at this attitude and corrected him, pointing out that she had done just as much to create the baby. However she knew it was a miracle that she had conceived.

It was amazing how everyone in the office just accepted the fact that Josephine and Leonard were an item, living together with a child on the way. Their friends looked at the situation as a fairy tale. At first it was not a difficult pregnancy for Josephine, although the morning sickness was a good reminder that she, not Leonard, was the one who was carrying the baby. It was only in the seventh month that she began to feel extremely exhausted. Some days she barely had the energy to get home after work and began to take the odd day off. On such occasions Leonard stepped into the breach and covered for her. It was obvious for the management that he was more than capable of running a section of the office.

Josephine went on maternity leave in the eighth month. She wrote to the company to say that she would like to take seven months off work, returning when the baby was six months old.

However, two weeks before the baby was born Leonard came home with a big grin on his face and a sparkle in his eye.

'I have got some brilliant news to tell you, Jo.'

'Have you?'

'Yes, I have got some extremely good news.'

'Go on then, what is it?'

'Well instead of being a supervisor,' he hesitated

'Yes?'

'...I have now been appointed a manager in the office. With all the perks. Brand new car and my salary's doubled.'

'That is brilliant news, but which section of the office?'

Leonard's expression suddenly changed and his smile became a frown.

'Oh, I thought you understood.'

'Understood what?'

'I'm now the manager in the office we both worked in. That's what I'm trying to tell you, they've made me the new manager in your office.'

'I'm happy about that but it will only be temporary until I come back.'

'No, I'm now the official manager.'

'I can't believe this. I wrote to the head office, explaining that I was going on maternity leave, and told them when I would like to return.'

'I know but they seem to think that it would be better if I took over now.'

'What, because you're a man?'

'That's a bit sexist, isn't it!'

'I don't understand,' Josephine muttered to herself.

'I think maybe they feel I'm more responsible, because of the way I stood by you.'

'Stood by me!'

'Yes ,of the condition that you're in.'

For once Josephine was lost for words.

'I suppose', said Leonard, they feel that maybe I would be the better person for the job. And anyway I would prefer you to stay at home with the baby until it's ready to go to school.'

This was something they had discussed but she realised that he was serious.

'You mean you want me to stay at home for five years?' She asked in astonishment.

'No children go to school full-time by the time they're four.'

'Oh four, five years, what's the difference? All I know is that it's too long for me to stay away from employment!'

'Don't worry about finance, Jo, because with this new job I'll be able to support you. I'll be earning enough for us both and will still be able to buy a new place.'

'How much are you earning then?'

When he told her the figure, she could not believe what she was hearing because it was substantially more than she had been getting for the same job. She also disliked Leonard's arrogance following this sudden financial rise. He even had the nerve to tell her that this new place would legally be his since he would be funding it, the sole bread winner.

There was only one consolation for her. Thank God, she thought, that although she was expecting his child, she was not married to this man.

Nine

She lay in bed that evening, completely disillusioned that the company for which she had worked so hard and long should offer her successor or temporary successor a higher salary than she had been earning. It was totally unfair. She was disillusioned too with Leonard. She should have never trusted him.

She only had herself to blame, for he hadn't shown his true character right at the start when he boasted about taking her job.

She could not blame him for the way it had happened because, whether consciously or subconsciously, she had planned the pregnancy. And if he had been playing a game with her, to some extent she had been doing the same with him. It was her who allowed their relationship to develop at such a pace. He was obviously smitten by the new Josephine and she had taken advantage of his interest. By first ignoring him and barely acknowledging his presence, she was more experienced than he was in the ways of the world. He was only his early twenties whereas she was in her mid-thirties.

If she was honest with herself, she had to admit that if she did not get pregnant now, then she never would, and she wanted a child more than anything in the world. If Leonard had an agenda she also had her own. Looking back on things, she wondered whether her interest in the young man had been entirely unselfish. Perhaps their whole relationship was based on deceit on both their parts.

They lay next to each other in bed, but he was absorbed by the television. Although she felt inwardly stressed, she managed to laugh out loud. He thought she had seen something amusing on the screen but in fact she was remembering past nights when they had laid side by side. She had been wondering whether that night was the night she would become pregnant. He had probably been eyeing the prospect of more money and longer holidays. For the moment she saw the funny side of it.

The pain she felt suddenly hit her again and she pulled the covers over her head, curled her legs up slightly and put her thumb in her mouth. It was sad that a woman of her age was sucking her thumb, but this was something she did on occasions when she was depressed. Leonard continued to watch the box and she dwindled into sleep. Later she woke up startled. The television was still on and she began to think about the prospect of having to stay at home for the next four years. No way, she said to herself. She felt the baby kick this reminded her that she would have to be strong to cope with the future. She must not give way to depression because this was no good for her and might affect the baby.

The following week she received a letter from the Head Office, confirming that they had decided to appoint Leonard their new manager in her place and suggesting that she would doubtless regard him as the best candidate for the post. There was no attention of either temporary or permanent status, and no reference to the fact that his salary was higher than hers, or any explanation.

The letter angered her but she did not want to think too much about it because the baby was due soon.

However, once the child was born a week later than expected, Josephine suffered with the baby blues. She had read about the condition in the baby book and knew that is was not uncommon. It was strange, nevertheless because giving birth and becoming a mum had been really exciting. Her family visited her and made her feel special, although they did not approve of the fact that she now had an illegitimate daughter.

The baby was beautiful and Josephine chose the name Adele for her. She thought in choosing a French name without any connection to anyone in her family or among her friends, she was striking out for freedom. This was her child and she would feel a sense of freedom every time she spoke her name.

Ten

The first four months after the arrival of Adele were exciting, although the baby blues got her down and led to occasional depression, despite the interest and support shown by friends and family. Leonard was quite delighted to be a father and Josephine could not believe how the birth of a daughter brought out the mature side of his personality or how helpful he suddenly became around the home.

The studio flat was far too small for all three of them and Josephine knew that eventually she would have to sell it. It was not just the effort that made her procrastinate. The idea of selling and letting Leonard buy a bigger place gave her a feeling of insecurity. For most of her adult life she had been independent. She had never been fully dependent on a man. The people stopped visiting to see the baby. It was then that Josephine realised that she was capable of fending for herself. Even though attitudes had improved she did not feel that Leonard understood her or her needs. If he did then he would not have expected her to stay at home full-time with the baby.

She began to see the negative side to their relationship and she became withdrawn, as she felt more depressed. In time the freedom that Leonard had slowly turned into resentment. Fatherhood had not changed his appetite for going and coming as he pleased. Leonard would often leave the house without telling her where he was going, or would say that he was going out for an hour and come home three hours later. And spent much of the weekends with his friends, leaving her alone with Adele. She said nothing to him, keeping her thoughts to herself, but gradually this resentment built up into a horrible self-revelation. Much as she adored her daughter, she sometimes regretted the fact that the baby had taken away her freedom.

The depression got worse, until one day she decided to relieve her tension by treating herself to a bottle of wine, which totally relaxed her. The following weekend she decided to buy something stronger, red wine that almost numbed her and gave her a false sense of well being. This drinking continued each and every weekend while Leonard was out with his friends. He must have known that she had begun to indulge herself with red wine, because she never hid the empty bottles. At the back of her mind it was not only the fact that Leonard still had a good social life, denied to her, but he had taken over her job, and was no longer financially independent.

As time went by, her weekend drinking extended to Monday mornings to help her cope with the week.

She had always been too busy with her career to bother about hobbies and never had time to be bored, but her whole life had changed. Leonard's habits got even worse. Instead of coming home immediately after work, he would go straight to the pub with his workmates. Josephine now started drinking every day as soon as the baby fell asleep. Although Leonard didn't seem to notice or to care, she no longer left the bottles around for him to find. He never caught her drinking because she usually made sure that she was in bed by the time he came home. Fortunately, Adele was a good sleeper and rarely woke at night, so Josephine was able to get plenty of rest, enabling her to recuperate easily from the drinking

By the time Adele was eight months old, Leonard had found a property he liked in Putney. He was earning enough to take out a mortgage on a house and although Josephine could have contributed from the proceeds of the eventual sale of the flat, he made it clear that the house was his and he obviously enjoyed this financial power. Whenever she brought up the subject of going back to work he said she should wait until Adele was at school. She could not bear the idea of waiting another three and a half years and in her mind she compromised by planning to return to work when Adele was two. Leonard wounded her quick on one occasion when he said that, if she still wanted a job when Adele went to school, he would be prepared to take her on. He had taken her job and now was offering her a position as his assistant!

She felt like a complete failure. She still had feelings for Leonard, but she could not fully express them due to the immense hurt he was causing her.

Her persistence eventually paid off. Soon after Adele's first birthday, Leonard agreed to pay for a child minder, and another managerial position, having spent so much time at home with a baby and also the drink, she had lost her confidence. However it took alot of courage, to return to her old place of work in junior position to the man who had replaced her[even if he was the father of her child]. She felt that work of any sort would do her good in the long run, until management offered her a more responsible position.

Unfortunately her drinking problem did not disappear with her situation. She became something of an addict. One particular Friday afternoon she and a few girls in the office went out to lunch together. She went over board and had one drink too many. On returning to work she slummed down in her chair, her face flushed, grinning into space. It was at that moment that Leonard walked into the room.

'Hi Leni,'she said

'Yes, Josephine,' said Leonard, gritting his teeth in embarrassment, for she was obviously the worse for wear. 'What do you want?'

'Nothing, why?'

'Nothing!'

'Yes, nothing. Josephine, you have been drinking?'

'What do you think? Tell me, Leonard, how can you not be doing anything tonight? You're normally out every Friday.'

'Josephine, would you please stop shouting?'

'Shouting, I'm not shouting!'

'You see what you've done,' he said angrily'

'What?'

'You're causing too much attention.'

'Oh is that all Leni, why did you...?'

'Josephine, I want you to get up and come to the office.'

'To the office, what on earth for?' she laughed.

He helped her get up and half dragged her towards the office.

'Josephine, what are you playing at?'

'Nothing, why?'

'Because, I'm going to have to ask you to leave the building.

'But why?'

'Because you're drunk!'

Josephine knew that Leonard was right and that she would have to go home, she decided then and there that she would not return. She could not face the ridicule.

Eleven

At first because he had important things to finish off in the office, Leonard was going to let Josephine go home on her own but, when she bumped into the office door on the way out, he knew that he could not leave her unaccompanied in such a state. He hailed a cab and went home with her. He helped her get undressed, and lay her in the bed.

He was worried about leaving her in that state, in case she threw up or maybe choked, so he rang work to let them know that he would not be back that afternoon. A situation like this could affect his job, and maybe his career. It was enough that word would inevitably spread that his girlfriend was drunk and he suddenly felt angry at her irresponsible conduct.

She was asleep and he looked at her with a mixture of contempt and remorse. He hated the way she had messed up his life. If she was so desperate for a baby, why couldn't she have chosen somebody else to fulfil her dream. Why not Paul, she's been with him long enough

Leonard did not know what to think. The whole situation was just too weird. For some reason Josephine had lost control over her mind and body. She must be carrying some great burden on her shoulders. He could not begin to understand but his anger suddenly turned to confusion and guilt.

What followed was almost surreal. Josephine was calling out in her dreams.

'No, don't' she shouted, 'I'll put them back. He'll never know.'

Her speech became slower.

'I didn't mean to take them, they'll never find out. Don't ask me where they are, they're in a safe place.'

Leonard could not make out every word but her voice became clear again.

'Where are you going? No, don't go in there. OK, I'll tell you where it is. It's in the wardrobe.'

'I hid it in a safe place,' Josephine continued, 'Where nobody would find it. You know where it is'

Leonard could not really believe what he was doing as he looked in the wardrobe. Some strange force had taken charge of him. In some uncanny way, someone in a deep sleep was giving him directions. But what he was looking for and where exactly would he find it?

'Look, I know about Taffy.'

The name was quite clear but whom or what was Taffy?

'Anyway the medical records are in there, I put them in that gold shoebox.'

Leonard found a shoe box right at the back of the wardrobe. Inside were the new shoes that Josephine had recently bought and that he so much liked. Beneath them was a layer of tissue paper, but there was nothing else. He was about to put the box back when he felt something soft underneath. When he investigated, he noticed that an envelope had been cleverly taped to the bottom.

He could not remember being so excited for years as he released the envelope and opened it. He was reminded of Christmas as a child, that same mixture of excitement and a slight pang of fear, because he did not know what to expect when he opened his presents. Now he unfolded what he thought were two letters, but which in fact was a letter and a medical record.

When he looked closely, he saw it related to Paul's medical records. He looked at the date at the top and saw that they were seven years old. Then he began to read it, with much difficulty. All he could make out were some key words such as 'low sperm count' and, vasectomy.' He could not understand the connection between the two. Maybe Paul was infertile and this was the reason why Josephine had decided to end their relationship.

It was then that things began to fall into place for him, her change in appearance, playing hard to get, agreeing for him to move in, and the suddenly finding herself pregnant. Perhaps this was all part of the plan, when she found out that Paul could not have children. Leonard felt severely hurt and deeply destroyed. He could not understand how he could have let himself fall into such a trap. Was he a fool that was a question he would definitely not ask his friends. What amazed him was the secretive side to Josephine's nature. She was always the one who was on about integrity but she had probably been deceiving him all the time.

He turned his attention back to the bed and observed her closely. She was still continuing her unconscious dialogue.

'I didn't mean to do it, was just something that I needed to know. 'I'm sorry.'

Then the word's ended abruptly and she fell into what was obviously a deep sleep.

Leonard placed the document back into the shoe box, but then realised that he had not read the accompanying letter. He took it out again. The words were all in large capitals:

NEVER MIND, WE WILL FIND A WAY TAFFY WILL HELP ME.

He wondered again who or what Taffy was. Was it a person or was it some drug perhaps?

Twelve

Josephine slept right through the night the following morning. Leonard remained with her, wondering if she would reveal any more information in her dreams. There was a big football match on television but he was nervous about disturbing her, and in any case there were more important things on his mind. He had long realised that Josephine had a drinking problem but until now it had not affected his dignity, and he now was concerned about how it might affect his daughter.

For sometime now he had thought of leaving but he was deeply distressed about Adele, and Josephine's capability to look after her. How had he got his life into such a muddle? Deep down, he knew he was much to blame because his ambition to succeed in business took precedence over everything else in his life, even Josephine and Adele. Sally came third. Although he was living with Josephine, who in turn never suspected that when he was late home from work he might be seeing somebody else. He had been very discreet in handling the situation and fortunately sally lived nearby.

Although he was dating Sally when he first met Josephine, he considered that they were both too young at the time for him to make any type of commitment. Even after the birth of Adele he kept in mind the possibility that they would live together in the future. In his mind he had thought of Sally as a long term girlfriend, to whom one day he might end up being married to. Josephine on the other hand was a short term- girlfriend whom he used to advance himself. He had never intended that relationship would last but the birth of Adele had altered the situation.

Deep down, he realised that Josephine's drinking may have arisen from an instinctive realisation that he did not truly love her, so he had to take some of the blame. Although he had taken advantage of her, she had done exactly the same with him. All she wanted was a child and their relationship was based on selfishness and deceit. There could be no future in it.

What amazed Leonard was that he had never been in a relationship where the female was as deceitful as he was. He had never been faithful to any woman but until now he had not considered the possibility that a woman could be unfaithful to him. For all he knew , innocent Sally may have been living a double life, although he doubted it. He thought he knew women, and could read their minds; but for the first time in his life he had to question his belief. If he broke off with Josephine, would he have the courage to come clean with Sally, to confess to her about Josephine and Adele? If so, would she think he could be trusted? He brushed his hands through his hair and sighed, trying to come to terms with his turbulent thoughts.

When Josephine eventually awoke, Leonard made her a cup of coffee and some toast before returning to the office. He telephoned her twice during the day to make sure she was alright. He arranged for his mother to pick Adele up from the child-minder and to look after her for the rest of the day to give Josephine the chance to recover fully. It was amazing that she had slept so long and so deeply. It was almost as though she had been in a trance, especially when she started talking in her sleep.

It was only after a few days had passed that he felt able to tell Josephine that their relationship would have to end. She felt quiet humiliated, because she too had wanted to end it and had been trying to find the right moment to tell him. He moved out that same evening to his mother's home, intending to pick up the rest of his things. Josephine assumed that he would provide financial support for their daughter.

A few days later Josephine had an unpleasant experience at the local hairdressing salon. The girl who was looking after her seemed to treat her with great animosity. She had attended to her before and she had almost found her most courteous. On this occasion she kept her waiting for thirty minutes before her hair was washed. Later when she was placed under the steamer, she found that the sides of her neck were beginning to burn. The temperature was much too high. There was a glass partition between where she was seated and where Sally and another hairdresser were busy chatting, their backs towards her. In desperation, she banged furiously on the glass. This finally brought Sally round to turn the temperature down.   'I'm sorry,' she said grudgingly.

There was definitely something odd but Josephine could not put her finger on it. Perhaps it was her imagination but she began to wonder if she was being deliberately mistreated when she noticed that all the customers were offered a cup of coffee apart from her.

'Is there anything wrong with me? ' asked Josephine.

The reply was totally expected.

'I am Leonard's girlfriend,' sally said, and I have been for six and a half years.'

Josephine looked shocked and could not believe her ears.

'You're Josephine, aren't you? I know because Leonard's told me all about you and your daughter, Adele.'

'Oh, what you mean is that you were Leonard's old girlfriend, before I met him?'

'I don't see how I can be anyone's old girlfriend. I'm only twenty.'

'Well, If Leonard's told you all about me and our daughter, you must know that I'm his girlfriend or was until we broke up recently.'

'Well you may be interested to know that he's been two -timing you. We've never stopped seeing each other.'

Josephine's world began to collapse around her. She could have understood if Leonard had returned to this spiteful girl who was deliberately trying to embarrass her but the idea that he had been seeing her the whole time was shocking. Perhaps it was untrue. But then she remembered all the times that he had come home late or stayed out at weekends, she began to accept reality'

Sally had deliberately provoked Josephine. She made sure that she would be looking after her when she came into the salon and had done everything to discomfort her. She had expected Josephine to go berserk, and was surprised at her cool reaction. The truth is that Josephine had reached a stage where she was fed up with disappointment she took them in her stride. If Leonard had really loved her, he would not have been unfaithful, He was younger than her and insecure, so perhaps she could even forgive him.

Sally was only a child. What did she know? Josephine did not feel threatened by her. Josephine was more sorry for her because she knew the road Sally would go down before discovering the truth about Leonard, perhaps about men in general. And felt very disappointed but philosophical about things. And not always been totally honest herself in important matters.

There was in fact one occasion when she had been very manipulative. She had actually broken into the doctor's surgery to find Paul's medical records at a time when the relationship with him was at very low ebb. It happened that her friend Cathy worked as a receptionist at the surgery. Visiting Josephine one evening, along with Barbara, Cathy placed a bunch of keys on the top of her handbag.

Doesn't it get confusing carrying all these keys around with you?' Josephine asked.

'No not really,' Cathy replied. 'There's only my house key, my car key and a couple of others, apart from the key I use to open the surgery, and I distinguish that by putting a green cap on it.

Josephine's ears pricked up . She knew from conversations with Paul that there was something medically wrong with him, but he always clammed up when she questioned him, and she had no idea whether it was serious. It could be the reason for the deterioration in their relationship. Here was an opportunity to discover the truth because he attended the surgery where Cathy worked. She hoped that if she borrowed the keys and found his medical records, she would be able to set her mind at rest.

When she thought about it, she couldn't believe how bold and decisive she was being at the time; it was as though she was somebody else. She did not even think about the consequences of her behaviour towards Cathy. As soon as she could do so without being noticed, she took the keys and placed them in her own handbag, then made an excuse to go out for a short time to buy some wine for dinner.

'Let me go' Barbara said. 'You can stay here with Cathy.'

'No, it's all right. You keep an eye on the lasagne and I'll go and come back quickly.

The surgery was quite near and with luck she could go there first, then buy the wine and be home within a short time, provided of course she could find Paul's file quickly. She felt awful as she inserted the green –capped key in the lock and entered the building. She had been to this surgery before and had seen a row of cabinets were her records were kept. She went straight for it. Every draw was marked alphabetically, so she knew where she wanted to look. Then she realised with horror that all the drawers were locked. In a panic she examined Cathy's bunch of keys. There were a couple of smaller ones and, miraculously, the first ones she tried fitted. Within minutes she had Paul's records in her hand.

Her heart was beating like a hammer and she was shaking. There was no time to read the papers on the spot. She closed the drawer, locked it and ran into the street. She hailed a cab that luckily came by and went to the wine shop. She decided to buy also a few items from a mini market, to justify her absence in case the girls thought she was taking a long time.

Fate was kind to her, and ten minutes later she was home. The whole operation had taken little over half an hour and neither Cathy nor Barbara thought anything of it. She replaced Cathy's keys, and heaved a great sigh. The rest of the evening was a nightmare. She had no appetite and could not eat, and she could not wait for the girls to go. Eventually she made an excuse of a headache, and they left early.

As soon as they had gone, she opened the file. One piece of information seemed to hit her in the eye. Paul was sterile. He had had a vasectomy six months before he and Josephine had met, and yet he had never said a word to her. How could he have been so deceitful? Whenever she had brought the subject of starting a family, he had always said he would think about it. In all that time, she had been unnecessarily on the pill. She had been cheated. Their whole relationship had been based on a lie. Her instinct about him had been correct.

A few weeks later she happened to bump into his mother. She assumed that the lady would know nothing about the vasectomy but she could not resist mentioning the matter, without of course explaining how she found out. I know it was so unfair to you and I was hoping and praying that he would eventually tell you the truth because I know how much you wanted children. The, trouble is Paul never wanted that sort of commitment.'

Thirteen

Josephine left the hairdresser's feeling worse than when she had entered, emotionally drained and disappointed with the hand life had dealt her. She bought three bottles of red wine on the way home. Although she had been warned recently by one of the doctors at the surgery to stop drinking, if not for the sake of her liver, then for the well being of her daughter. She knew this was good advice but it did not make things easier when she discovered that another man had been dishonest with her, first Paul with his vasectomy and now Leonard, who had been carrying on with sally behind her back.

Josephine would soon have to leave her home and did not know how she could face the future. If a few glasses of wine could help her forget her misery for a few hours, what was the harm?

When she arrived home, she sat in a chair and silently wept, feeling hopeless. She rang her mother to ask if she could look after Adele until the next day. That evening she thoroughly indulged herself with red wine, and also took several tablets for a headache.

The following morning rolled into the afternoon, the afternoon into the evening. The phone had rang many times that day, but if she heard it, she lacked the energy to answer it. Her mother knew something was wrong, and when she could get no reply to her call, she visited the house, taking Adele with her. There was no response when she rang the bell and knocked on the door, although she could hear the television. With the growing alarm, she decided to ring Leonard until she realised that he would no longer be at the office at that hour, so she telephoned the police.

A police car arrived within minutes and she explained the situation to the officers.

'Josephine, your mother is very concerned about you, could you please open the door. 'Josephine, Josephine!'

There was still no reply, so one of the policemen began to kick the door down. By chance, Leonard arrived at that very moment the door gave way and the officers ran into the house.

'What on earth is going on?' he asked. 'And what is Adele doing here?'

Josephine's mother started to explain, but was interrupted by one of the policeman.

'Mrs. Harry' he said.

The tone in his voice left no doubt that something was seriously wrong. Josephine's mother told Leonard to look after Adele and rushed to her daughter's side. She quickly put her hands over her mouth.

'What on earth has happened to her?' she said in a muffled voice.

'Josephine, Josephine, can you hear me?' said the officer, shaking her and slapping her face. 'Josephine, it's your mother, wake up, Adele's here.'

There was still no response, and he checked for a pulse.

'Her pulse is very week. We'd better call for an ambulance,' he said.

Ten minutes later the ambulance was there. While they waited, the policeman looked around and found three empty bottles of red wine and a half- full bottle of pills.

They seemed to wait an eternity. At last a nurse appeared and addressed Mrs. Harry.

Took Mrs. Harry and Adele to the hospital, where they waited for news.

'I was always against you and Josephine living together and having children before getting married,' Mrs. Harry told him, not so much as a criticism but because she needed to say something.

Leonard realised that she would probably want to blame someone, and he was the obvious choice. He no longer had any loving feelings for Josephine but he was in shock, and worried that she might die. As he gazed into space, he heard Mrs. Harry continuing to criticise his relationship with Josephine and it was obvious that she had no idea that they had broken up'.

They seemed to wait an eternity. At last a nurse appeared and addressed Mrs. Harry.

'Would you follow me please.' she said

'Shall I come too?' asked Leonard.

'No, you stay here.' Mrs. Harry said a voice that would provoke no argument.

She followed the nurse into a small room, clutching onto the buggy in which Adele was fast asleep.   'Would you sit down?'

'No, I'll be fine.'

'I'm sorry, Mrs. Harry, but your daughter died a few minutes ago.'

Now Mrs. Harry did sit down, slowly.

'But I don't understand,' she said, 'how, why?'

'Did your daughter drink alot?'

'No, not that I know.' Mrs. Harry could just about get the words out.

'She may have had liver failure.'

'I just can't believe she's dead, my Josephine!' Tears slowly began to fall down her cheek. The nurse comforted her by resting her hand on her shoulder.

'Is there anything that I can get you, or anybody that you want me to ring?'

'No, it's alright.' She got a handkerchief from her handbag and wiped her face. She took a deep breath and sighed, sucked her bottom lip and then rose up energetically from her seat.

'Thank you, nurse, don't worry, I'll be fine.'

The nurse held the door open for her and Adele. Leonard was waiting anxiously.

'Is everything alright?' he asked.

'As if you really care.'

'What's that supposed to mean?'

'Well, you didn't look after her, did you?'

'What I'm trying to tell you is that Josephine is dead.'

'What!'

'Yes, she died of liver failure. They said that she must have been drinking too much, and I wonder why.'

'What you're saying is it's my entire fault.'

'Exactly. You were never around when she needed you.'

'Did Josephine tell you that?'

'No, but somehow I knew things weren't right between you, but I just didn't want to get involved. I hoped you two would sort your own problems out.'

Leonard stayed silent. He knew that Josephine had been drinking but he felt that it was unfair to put all the blame on him. Josephine was a grown woman and she should have handled her own problems better. Why could she not have been more responsible? And now who was going to take care of Adele?

Fourteen

Adele went home with her grandmother. Although Leonard knew that it would be a sign of maturity if he offered to look after her, he knew also that Josephine's heartbroken parents would never agree to such an arrangement, especially since they blamed him for their daughter's death. In any case he was far too young and inexperienced to care for a young child, whatever arrangements he could make to help. He did not want the responsibility anyway. It would take away his freedom.

A week after the funeral, the reading of Josephine's will took place at her parent's house. Apparently she had made a new will after the birth of Adele and had updated it very recently. Leonard was invited and had some expectations of benefiting from a life policy that he knew Josephine had taken out. On arrival, he found Mr. And Mrs. Harry and Josephine's brother Marlon, whom he had never met. He was tall, with pitch- black hair, piercing blue eyes and a rosy complexion. There was an amazing resemblance to Adele.

To Leonard's astonishment, Paul arrived shortly afterwards. Surely Josephine could not have left him anything? In fact Paul had his own expectations, something perhaps to do with the flat they had shared which he so generously gave her and which he learnt had been rented out since she had moved in with Leonard to a large place.

After refreshments, Mr. Harry gathered everyone present around him and began to read the will. It transpired that Josephine had left more money than Leonard or Paul could have supposed. They were both surprised to learn that she had considerable savings, which she never touched, as well as two cars, which she never used and which were in the garage in Putney. The substantial part of her estate was left to Adele and there were bequests for her parents and her brother, Marlon.

Leonard and Paul were beginning to wonder why they had been invited. In fact they were last to be mentioned in the will.

Josephine left Leonard a poem she had written about honesty. She left Paul a birdcage containing a budgerigar, with a letter in explanation:

'You've always liked birds, so I thought I'd leave you my budgie. Her names Adrian. I bought her a few months ago but decided to leave her at mums because her crying disturbed Adele. I'm sure you'll love her. There's a booklet of how to take care of her underneath the cage.'

Leonard left the room in order to calm down while Paul sat there in shock. Josephine's parents had gone to great pains to ensure that he would be present for the will reading, telephoning him at work to remind. He felt a complete fool.

'Well, you must admit Josephine had a great sense of humour,' said Leonard on his return, making the best of the situation.

Fifteen

One of the most important provisions in Josephine's will was a bequest of money and her cars to her brother Marlon, with the request that he take responsibility for looking after Adele. This was something that Leonard was likely to fight. He was too young and selfish too bring up a child. Marlon was a deliberate choice. He was the apple of his parent's eye and as far as they were concerned he could do no wrong. Josephine had never understood why they had favoured her brother and she decided that, rather than leave them to look after her daughter, she would put her brother to the test. It could be the making of him.

Whether or not she had been thinking clearly with Adele's best interest in mind, Mr and Mrs. Harry thought her idea was a good one. The only problem was that Marlon did not feel any more ready for such responsibility than Leonard. To start with, he was unmarried, although he had a steady girlfriend called Andrea, but he could not be sure how she would react to the idea of helping to raise a young child. He was particularly fond of travel, but having Adele around would seriously affect his mobility and might put an end to anything more than an annual holiday. His image as a world traveller was at risk and he would no longer be able to brag to his friends about the exotic countries he had visited. He enjoyed a racy life.

He was, however, very good with children. Josephine had noticed how much love he had shown to an ex- girlfriend's daughter to whom he had tried to be a good stepfather. He liked kids and this was another reason for her choice of him as the best person to care for Adele. After an initial hesitation, he began to see a positive side to the task he had inherited. He spoke to Andrea, and he was very pleased when she agreed willingly that Adele should move in with them. Somewhat to Marlon's surprise, she welcomed the idea and respected him for wanting to accept the responsibility. In a curious way, it made him more attractive to her. Any doubts she kept to herself.

It was Andrea, more than Marlon, who had realised the full implications of having a child in the house. Marlon worked in advertising, which meant that he spent much of his own time away from home. Andrea was a model, much favoured by makers of sportswear, bikinis and underwear . She was Brazilian origin, tall, slim and very attractive, with long wavy hair and captivating brown eyes. They made a great couple, and shared similar interest, such as travelling, jazz music and dining out. All that might have to change but in any case Josephine had left Marlon money and he could always sell the cars if necessary

Marlon saw the legacy as a windfall and proposed to celebrate by going on holiday to St. Lucia, the small Caribbean island. Andrea had never been there and it would give them both an opportunity to bond with Adele. He might not have the chance again to travel so far for some time. The idea appealed to Andrea, who was able to take time off from her free lance work, but she made it clear that she was not prepared to be left holding the baby while Marlon went off and enjoyed himself. He thought she would automatically become a devoted mother, but he should have realised that she was his girlfriend and not his wife, that Adele was his blood relative and not hers, and that it was his responsibility to look after the child. This did not mean that she would not play her part but if she was going on holiday, she wanted it to be a holiday.

Due to the circumstances, Marlon hired a nanny at great expense for the full eight weeks they were away. It was like a dream come true for Marlon and Andrea. They were used to travelling, but this was usually in relation to their jobs and they rarely travelled together. When they did, they could only stay away for a couple of days at the most.

Even on holiday, there were times when Andrea found it difficult to accept Adele. She was a beautiful child, with jet black hair, amazing deep blue mirror glass eyes, and pale rosy skin that radiated good health. What startled Andrea was that Adele was the spitting image of Marlon. He was incredibly handsome and had a good masculine stature tall, broad shoulders, slime waistline and long legs. As he always dressed well, this made him stand out all the more. Most strangers assumed because of the resemblance ,Adele was in fact his daughter. He obviously enjoyed the extra attention he received as the presumed father of such a lovely child. If people assumed that Andrea was the mother, they did not realise that, although one day she wanted to settle down and have children that time had not arrived she was still too interested in her modelling career.

The villa they stayed in was exquisite and beautiful decorated from top to bottom in cream, which was Andrea's favourite colour. They spent the daylight hours exploring the beautiful island, swimming and sunbathing, although Marlon preferred to stay in the shade because of his pale skin. Andrea and Marlon were able to leave the nanny in charge of Adele while they went dancing at night. They enjoyed themselves thoroughly.

When the holiday came to an end, they returned to London and tried to get back into their own routine. This was impossible with Adele. The nanny had been employed for two months only and Andrea was not anxious to spend all her time acting as a mother.

'When are we going to get another nanny? She asked only after a few days when Marlon had taken no steps to find someone.

'I quite liked the nanny we had,' he said. 'I'll call the agency later and find if she'll be willing to work full-time.'

They then discussed the merits of having a live-in nanny or someone who would come in the morning and leave at night, or if they were very lucky a person who would be available whenever they needed her when they both wanted to travel, for instance. They both were completely inexperienced in this sort of manner.

They had a stroke of luck. The nanny they had taken to ST. Lucia had formed an attachment to Adele and was pleased to be offered permanent employment in their house. Her name was Beatrice and she soon became part of the family. She was good at her job and Marlon was quite content to leave the child in care whenever he or Andrea were away. She was short and looked both sensible and respectable. These qualities were reflected in the sober way she dressed. She had a very pleasant voice and set an example for a young child. Much to her surprise Andrea began to feel a little jealous, of Beatrice and wondered if she was right to concentrate on her career and having fun. Andrea was beginning to see the attractions of motherhood, but when she gave the matter more serious thought she realised that she valued her independence too much. Her earning power was important to her and would never want to become too dependent on a man. Being stuck in a house and unable to move or have the freedom to do what she wanted was not something she was ready for. In five years' time perhaps, when she was thirty, she might think differently. Marlon would be thirty-five by then and Adele would be seven. But would they still be together in five year's time? She considered that she was better off as things stood. The future could take care of itself.

In fact, she was forced to take the decision two years later when Marlon proposed to her. Adele had reached the age of four, and watching her develop had encouraged him to want to start a family of his own. Another child would be a lovely companion for her. Andrea did not see things in quite the same way. Although at first the idea attracted her, she realised that the only reason Marlon had proposed to her was because he wanted to start a family, not because he loved her. She could foresee a glum future in which the, children came first in his affections.

She had known women who had married men whose main concern was to start a family. These men always loved the children more than their wives, who often felt miserable and unwanted, especially when they found themselves doing all the hard work while the husbands left the children in their care and were free to go off and do exactly what they wanted. No way did she want to be caught in such an unbearable situation.

After much thought she decided to end the relationship with Marlon. It was not easy because he automatically assumed that another man was involved. He could not simply understand that she just wanted to be loved and appreciated for herself, not as someone to give him a baby. To marry for love was something, to marry to start a family was another matter. That sort of marriage often ended with the man becoming bored and talking to another woman, explaining that his wife didn't understand him, and then starting an affair. Perhaps she was being negative, but there was some truth in her thinking. It was very sad but she felt that she had to end their relationship and move on rather than make a major decision that could ruin her life.

Marlon tried to change her mind, but in the end he had no other choice then to let her go, with much regret on his part. The experience taught him one lesson; he did not really understand how a woman's mind worked. This rather soured his personality.

Sixteen

At first Marlon bitterly regretted losing Andrea, although she was never the perfect mother figure for Adele. He had come home one evening when Beatrice was out to find Adele dining on choc-ice and chips. He would have been even more startled if he knew she had lunched on ham and crisps. Despite Andrea's faults, however, he could not easily put her out of his mind.

In due course he became interested in another woman. He did not spend much time looking for the perfect person and he came across Dixie in a wine bar on a singles night. She was no match for Andrea in looks or personality but was very pretty and would probably be a better mother for Adele. She had long wavy brown hair, brown eyes and olive complexion. Dixie was only five foot four inches and always wore high heels to make her look taller. She had a good figure but had to pay special attention to what she ate because she put weight on very easily. She was an altogether more motherly person than Andrea and soon established an excellent relationship with Adele. The little girl was very fond of Dixie and delighted when Marlon finally married her'

Unfortunately it was not a marriage made in heaven. Marlon married Dixie because he loved her he saw her as a person suitable to help raise Adele. At times he showed more consideration for Beatrice the nanny and Dixie did not feel she was mistress in her own home. She found that whenever she tried to talk to Marlon he never understood her point of view. This lead to alot of anger and frustration on her part. The arguments grew more and more frequent and, although she knew it would hurt Adele, Dixie decided that she must leave Marlon. There was no future living with a man who did not really love her and found fault with her. She walked out, leaving him a note.

When Marlon read the note, he thought it was all for the best and did not especially regret Dixie's departure. Marlon would simply resume the life he had enjoyed before he met her, and in any case there was no one better than Beatrice to look after Adele. The loss of Dixie was more upsetting to the little girl, who had begun to grow quite close to her, but Marlon assumed she would soon get over it.

There was a sting in the tail, six months later Dixie wrote to Marlon to tell him that she was pregnant and was expecting his baby shortly. A child of his own was what he really wanted and he would never have been so unconcerned about her departure if he had known that she was carrying his baby. Surely she must have known that she was pregnant when she walked out on him?

This changed everything as far as he was concerned and he asked Dixie to return home. She knew he only wanted her home because of the baby so she refused. When little Lucy was born, he was at the hospital begging Dixie to go home with him. Although she was emotionally weak, she had the strength to say no again. She knew that he didn't love her or respect her and she could envisage a situation where if she went back, she would be playing second fiddle to Beatrice. Marlon would, certainly have more love for his child than his wife. It had been the same with Adele and she was only his niece.

Adele was already seven by the time Lucy celebrated her first birthday, and she was old enough to observe the change in her uncle's behaviour. He had become increasingly depressed about not being able to see his daughter as often as he wanted. He began to drink more and gamble in clubs and at home sometimes with his friends. Beatrice too became worried as she saw how depressed he had become. His whole personality had changed and he no longer spent much time with Adele, who asked Beatrice what she had done wrong because her uncle no longer talked or played with her. Beatrice did not know what to say except that he was probably missing his wife and daughter.

'Why doesn't Uncle Marlon ask Dixie and Lucy to come home then?'

'I don't know, maybe they don't want to come home.'

'But why?'

Beatrice didn't know how to handle the situation except to carry on as if everything was normal.

Things got worse before they got better. Marlon lost far more then they could readily afford gambling, and for a time he was too depressed even to go back to work. He eventually picked himself up, after a period of feeling sorry for himself, and got some stability back into his life. If it had not been for the remarkable Beatrice, Adele's life would have been very unhappy.

Her uncle was always very miserable on Lucy's birthday the occasions when he saw her. Adele kept hoping that she would be allowed to accompany him on one of the visits, but this never seemed to happen. As the years went by, the possibility grew more remote, and her relationship with her uncle did not improve. She once criticised Marlon to Mrs. Harry, but much as her grandmother loved her, she seemed not to believe her. Marlon could do no wrong in his mother's eyes, and this prevented Adele from being close to her grandparents as she might have been. In fact it was only her nanny who seemed to understand her.

When Adele was fourteen and a half, she began to have pains in her lower abdomen. She had no idea what was causing them and Beatrice explained she was becoming a woman and would soon start her menstrual cycle. The fact that she would have to menstruate every month for the next forty years scared her, but the thought that she was growing up gave her a sense of excitement. When Beatrice told Marlon, he seemed to detest being around Adele.

She could still remember the affection her uncle had once shown her but, now that she was on the threshold of womanhood, he seemed almost indifferent to her. This made her horribly insecure and fearful of living in a house without love. She knew that she had Beatrice, but for how long? Her uncle could fire the nanny whenever he chose. Perhaps he would decide that she was old enough to look after herself.

What had caused such a change in his attitude? There was a time when he had loved her but, of course that was true of Andrea and Dixie also, and where were they now? She had become quite close to them until Uncle Marlon decided to get rid of them. Or was it the other way round? Her heart raced as she became more aware of the uncertainty of her future. Was this life, falling in and out of love and then deciding to move on when things got difficult or when you got bored not caring if, for your own selfish reasons, you hurt the other person or even the children involved? This adult game just didn't make any sense at all.

How on earth was she ever going to trust a man.? Weren't you supposed to get married, have children and then live happily ever after? Or was this just a fairytale, an adult version of Father Christmas? Why did life have to be such a let down? Why on earth was her uncle making her life such a misery? It wasn't fair. She would have liked to discuss these matters with her grandparents but they did not seem to understand her worries.

A subtle change occurred in her attitude towards Beatrice. Adele wanted to be less dependent on her in case she decided to go and work for someone else or in case her uncle thought that a growing girl no longer needed a nanny. It was a matter of not wanting to get hurt, just in case Beatrice was no longer around. In fact because Uncle Marlon was often away on business or worked late, Beatrice was still needed.

Beatrice was wonderfully understanding and was aware instinctively of what was worrying Adele. On one occasion she knocked on the door and asked if she could come in. She sat at the end of the bed.

'You're so lucky, Adele,' she said.

'Lucky, why do you say that?'

'Because you've got your whole life ahead of you, and bright new things will eventually shine in your life.'

'What do you mean?'

'One day you will fully understand what I'm saying.'

Adele remained silent and looked towards the light from the lamp beside her bed. She loved the way she had been allowed to decorate her bedroom. She painted the walls an ivory colour, and put a poster on her wall of Peter Andre, who she adored. She bought the lamp from the local store. It had a frosted glass shade, finished off with an antique stem. She also had a peach ceramic table-lamp on a side table, to match her quilt and pillowcase. There was a pinewood bookcase on one side of the room, and a small desk on the other, and a small multi-coloured sofa bed in front of the bed in which she slept and on which Beatrice was now sitting.

Adele knew that she was fortunate to live in such surroundings, even if there was less love in the house that she needed. She also knew that she was lucky to have Beatrice

'I always want you to remember, 'Beatrice told her, 'that no matter what happens I will always love you.'

'What do you mean, what's going to happen?' Adele was suddenly alarmed.

'Nothing,' Beatrice reassured her, 'but you're growing up into a beautiful young woman. I know you're only fourteen but I remember when I was fourteen and it only seems like yesterday. You won't need a nanny forever, and one –day I'll have to move on. But not just yet.'

When Beatrice left her room, Adele lay down and stretched her whole body, relieving the tension. She felt safe within her own room, and Beatrice's words had comforted her. She relaxed into sleep.

She awoke suddenly when she heard her uncle calling her urgently.

'Adele, Adele!' he came storming into her room.

'Yes., Uncle,' she said.

'Did you see the casserole dish today?'

'Yes. I needed to warm up the stew in the oven? You can just quickly warm it in a pot. You must also remember to wash up afterwards.'

'Yes. I know but...'

'But nothing! What you need to remember, young girl, is to show me a little respect by doing what you're told'

'But Uncle...'

'No Adele, I'm just sick and tired of all your excuses. You're just a good for nothing!'

'What have I done that's so terrible?'

'I just said you need to learn to respect me and that means not answering me back. Do you hear me?'

'Yes ,Uncle.'

'Or maybe you don't understand because I know you find it difficult to understand things, don't you?'

'No, why?'

'Why, why, because if I tell you to do something you never do it, it's like you just don't listen!'

'But, Uncle, I do.'

It was then that he made an extraordinary statement;

'I'm not surprised Andrea and Dixie left me,' he said. It was because of you, you know.'

Adele was dumbstruck.

'I've never told you this before,' he continued. 'You have spoilt alot of plans in my life. I could have done so much more if I didn't have to look after you!

'I thought you loved me, Adele said. She was now in tears. 'I thought you loved my mother.'

'You were part of a deal,' was his cruel reply.

'Uncle...' she tried to speak.

'I'm tired,' he said, 'I've had a hard day and just don't have the time to listen to you. I'm off to bed. I'll see you in the morning!'

He left the room; leaving Adele huddled up on the bed, crying profusely. The contented feeling following her brief conversation with Beatrice now was gone. She had nothing but fear and hatred in her heart.

Seventeen

The situation worsened and within a few months Marlon let Beatrice go. He blamed his financial circumstances but the real reason was that he was no longer willing to pay for her. As far as he was concerned, Adele had turned fifteen and was able to look after herself.

Without the love of her former nanny, Adele felt totally alone. She was not receiving the type of fatherly love and direction that she needed from her uncle, and her grandparents would hear no word of criticism of him. Adele was left feeling empty and with very little self-respect. Perhaps it was a small wonder that she took up with a man ten years her senior. Despite her tender years, she was quite willing to begin a sexual relationship in return for some sort of love and regard, but she was never willing to give Simon her heart. She had been too hurt by people disappearing from her life as soon as she had begun to trust and love them.

Simon was kind and caring, but could not see herself being with him forever. He was blonde, tall, six foot two and very slim with green eyes that stood out a mile. He was in many ways completely different from her uncle, which may have been why she found him desirable. He had a great sense of humour that was a total contrast to Marlon's dour contempt. He worked in the West End, in a market research department. The job paid well and allowed him to live a decent life.

By the second year of their relationship, Adele found herself pregnant. She was still young, but at seventeen old enough to get married. Although she did not want to make that sort of commitment if there was any practical alternative. She had deliberately kept the relationship secret because she knew that her uncle would not have been happy about her dating a man ten years older.

She dreaded the embarrassment of telling him the news but knew she had no choice. To her amazement he did not react as she had expected. Indeed he seemed pleased that someone with a good job and earning power was willing to take her off his hands. It was as though he was happy that she had got herself pregnant, and he assumed automatically that she would marry Simon.

'So have you both worked out when you'll get married?' he asked.

'Married, who said anything about getting married?'

'What do you mean, isn't that your intention?'

'No, why should it be?'

'Because you're pregnant!'

'I don't want to get married.'

'Why not?'

'Because I don't want to tie myself up for life I'm only seventeen.

'What's the point of getting married just because I'm pregnant?'

'And it will lead to divorce when I get bored.'

He thought for a moment, unable to understand how this young girl could turn down marriage if it was offered.

'What?'

'So what are you going to do?'

'Have the baby and bring it up here.'

'What!' He was startled by her reply.

'Well, this is my home, isn't it?' she asked.

'I suppose so,' he agreed reluctantly, 'but you can't stay here forever.

It's about time you started thinking about your own accommodation. You're old enough to have a baby so you're old enough to be independent. He realised that she wasn't aware that her mother had left her a flat, which she could inherit when at the age of twenty-one.

Her uncle's mood swings did not help Adele through her pregnancy. At one time he did not talk to her for three weeks, for no apparent reason. She found it very confusing and dispiriting. She would come home from college, or sometimes from the hospital, anxious to share her experiences of the day, but on rare occasions he was at home and he would simply ignore her. At other times she would wait for her return. His routine then was to get a can of beer from the fridge and telephone one of his friends. They would often talk animatedly for twenty minutes or more. The energy and expression of laughter in his voice contrasted sharply with the lack of enthusiasm with which he barely acknowledged his niece's existence. Sometimes if she was watching a film on television, he would switch to the sports channel without a word of apology. He behaved as though she disgusted him.

She decided to come home early and prepare a special meal for him. He returned at seven O'clock to find the table laid in the dining room. When she called him to dinner, he took one look at the food and walked out of the house, without so much as a word. He did not return until ten-thirty, well over three hours later'

When he did begin to talk to her, he would repeat that she was no good and that Simon was just using her, for what he could get. She was surprised therefore when he actually initiated a conversation one Saturday evening, while she was watching a film.

'Have you thought how you are going to support yourself and your child?' he asked.

'Simon will help, and I'm sure I'll be entitled to some government benefits.'

'You've got it all planned, haven't you? So you're going to extract money out of Simon and the government. That's very clever isn't it?'

'What else do you expect me to do? You're not offering to help.'

'You should of thought of the consequences before sleeping with Simon. It's not my responsibility. In fact I'm getting fed up with you in my house. Why don't you go and stay with your fancy man? You can sponge off him, and not off me.

These comments really hurt Adele. What was a pregnant girl of seventeen to do? She had no money and had to seek help wherever she could find it. She did not regard that as sponging. If she could afford to leave, or find some way to exist independently, she would be out of the house and away from her uncle like a shot. Living in such a stressful atmosphere was no good either for her or the baby she was carrying. She was not strong enough to face life in a new and strange place.

It amazed her how so many people in the neighbourhood loved Marlon. He was such a friendly man, to everyone but her. Her grandparents could not believe that he could be a complete monster where she was concerned. His public face was completely different from the one he displayed to her at home. There were even occasions when he assaulted her physically. Once, when he disagreed with something she said, he lashed out, hitting her on the head. It was not too severe a blow but his behaviour was very frightening and humiliating. He followed her up the stairs one day, complaining that she was walking too slowly and pulling her hair until she let him pass. The treatment left her feeling unwanted, useless and worthless. She began to think that there was no such thing as love in the world, only selfishness, and this made her question Simon's regard for her. She was too intimidated to seek his protection.

Her uncle's cruel behaviour was totally confusing. Where had the love gone? What had she done to him? She had no idea what she could do, but unless he threw her out on the street, she would remain in the house until the child was born. She could not see beyond that for the time being. If she had realised the consequences, she might have been more careful about becoming pregnant, but she was responsible for the child inside her and would fight to make its life better than hers.

Money was the main priority, providing Simon paid for their child's basic needs, she hoped she could manage without having to rely on her uncle. As soon as she was able to work, she was determined to earn her own living, but she was not at all experienced in the ways of the world there was no one to whom she could turn to for advice, now that Beatrice was no longer around. In any case she did not want to bother her.

Due to all the pressure, Adele gave birth to a beautiful baby girl three weeks early. She had deep black hair and piercing blue eyes and it was obvious that she was her mother's daughter. They looked very much alike. Adele named her Josephine, after her mother. Any doubts she had during pregnancy vanished with the birth. It was as though a miracle had taken place in her life. She looked at motherhood as a complete blessing. The privilege of bringing a new and beautiful person into the world justified all her suffering.

She had felt great being in hospital but this feeling disappeared when she looked outside the window. From being warm and secure, she felt sad and lonely because she did not trust Simon, and her uncle no longer loved her. Simon visited her, it is true, but more out of duty than love, and she became very aware that she had no close friends.

Marlon came to collect her and the baby from the hospital and he set up the cot in her bedroom. As time went by, he got used to the situation but made it very clear that he did not like it. He became more and more disrespectable to her, telling her more than once that he was disgusted that she had an illegitimate baby. Worse still, he called her a bad mother and a parasite because she accepted financial support from Simon. That was all the money she got, and she was surely entitled to it, but not in her uncle's eyes.

This particular insult hurt the most, especially when he said that she had probably got pregnant on purpose to get money from Simon.

'Don't you have any respect for yourself? He asked. 'Look at you! You call yourself a mother. Couldn't you have waited until you had your own flat? You're mad anyway. That's why Simon doesn't want to marry you. Fancy marrying a mad woman. You can't even cook. Every time you cook something it burns. I'm surprised that you can feed your baby probably, poor kid.'

When he said these terrible things there was disgust on his face, as though she was the lowest of the low. The only thing that kept her sane was a day-to- day routine of taking Josephine out for walk, enjoying the interest strangers took in the baby. The friendly smiles from passers- by were in stark contrast to her uncle's unfriendly demeanour. People she did not know treated her with respect and acknowledged her right to exist and be happy. This kept her alive and created a little bit of peace in her life.

Eighteen

Adele knew that she had to break free from her uncle's chains as soon as she could. He was doing nothing but damaging her life, and she did not want her daughter to grow up in such an unhappy environment, as it could prove very harmful to her. It was not long before she started looking for somewhere else to live. She decided to find a place and then worry about how to pay for it. Adele wanted to get away from Putney, where she had been brought up, and something kept telling her to look for accommodation in Mitcham. She could not explain the urge but it seemed like fate when, within a few weeks, she found a place that she liked in that area. It was like a one- bedroom flat, but it was spacious, well designed and very comfortable. When she told her uncle, he didn't believe her and then, to her amazement, he then seemed to want her to stay with him in Putney. Perhaps he did feel guilty but she was determined to stay away from him. She needed what little money Simon was able to provide for her day-to- day living, so she applied for housing benefit. As an unmarried mother with a small baby, her application was apparently treating her with some priority, it was red-letter day in her life when the benefit was granted and she was able to pay a deposit on the new flat and move in with Josephine.

By this time her little girl was six months old, Adele knew that her daughter felt secure in the new environment. It was Adele who was the one feeling insecure. Although she no longer had to endure her uncle's bad temper and criticism, her life now was monotonous since she was stuck constantly in the flat with her daughter. She decided to look for a part time- job that she could do from home, if only to prove to Marlon that she was not a parasite. At least it would bring a little variety into her life

In the meantime, she took every possible opportunity to leave the flat daily and explore the area. Something must have drawn her to Mitcham. It had a historical feel about it, and she got to know the area well and all the small roads. She loved the spacious beautiful cricket green, and when she first came across Love Lane, was convinced that she had been there before.

One afternoon Adele came across a job advertised in the local paper. A clothes agency was looking for people who wanted to earn extra money in their spare time. All that was required was to sell clothes on commission from a small catalogue. On enquiry, it was explained to her that most of the company's agents left the brochures with local householders and later called again to collect orders. It was not a secure job but something she could easily do while looking after Josephine. Although she did not have a car, she was already becoming very familiar with the local streets and had some idea of where potential customers might live. The only problem, she was told, was that most people paid in cash for the goods they ordered. The agency was more concerned about being able to trust her with cash then about her security or about where she would keep the cash until she was able to return the payments back to the company, having run a police check to establish that she didn't have a criminal record, they took her on.

She decided to start with the block of flats close to where she lived, and then gradually further afield. Taking Josephine with her, she carried the catalogues in a bag, which she hung on the buggy. She delivered them wherever she could and said she would pick them up in two days' time, giving potential customers enough time to look through them. She did her work methodically and speedily.

She knew she had to remain strong for Josephine and found that the neighbourhood where she worked gave her an inner confidence. She especially loved Figgs Marsh with its beautiful trees lined alongside the road. She felt curiously at peace there and strangely hopeful, as if something good was in store for her. Some evenings she would leave Josephine with a friendly neighbour and walk across Figgs Marsh. She knew it was dangerous because it was dark, but somehow she felt as though she was being protected. She had often had this feeling recently. Her uncle had dug a big hole for her and she had been in danger of falling in and never being able to climb out, but something had saved her. In fact, she had almost dug another pit for herself in getting pregnant by someone with whom she did not really want to have a long-term relationship. She remembered the time when her uncle had suggested that she get rid of the baby who now was her pride and joy. Something had made her rebel against such a decision. It was as though she had a guardian angel.

She knew instinctively that there was more to life than money, even though she was not finding it easy to live on her income, provided she had a minimum to look after herself and Josephine. She had been saved from falling into a hole but was still at risk, but now she was trying seriously to sort her life out and she realised that success or failure was down to her.

Yet she still needed help but not the sort of help that Simon or the local authority could provide, she did not want to end up like her mother. Adele needed wise guidance, and out of the blue she received a letter from Beatrice. Her old nanny had gone to the trouble of tracking her down. Beatrice was a good friend, to hear from her suddenly was like a miracle.

She wrote that she was working with a family in Esher, looking after two little boys aged three and four but she was shortly due a holiday and would love to come and spend a week with Adele. Adele could not have been more excited, and wrote back immediately. She could hardly wait for the day to arrive when she would again see her old friend. Adele was sure she could arrange things so that there was enough room in her flat.

The two women had so much to talk about. The concern on Beatrice's face was obvious when Adele told her all about the hurt and anxiety her uncle had caused, the birth of Josephine and about how she was now living.

'Tell me about Simon.' Beatrice said.

'Oh, I think I chose to be with an older man because I was trying to combine a father figure with a boyfriend, but things just didn't work out.'

'That's what I thought because it has been difficult for you, Adele. You didn't know your mother died when you were very young. Then you suffered verbal abuse from your uncle in your mid-teens.'

That summed up her life rather well, Adele thought. Verbal abuse, was that what you called it? And there was some physical abuse as well!'

'You've done well, though,' Beatrice continued, at least you were brave enough to have the baby.'

Later in the day, when she had unpacked, showered and made herself comfortable, Beatrice was bouncing Josephine on her knee.

'She's so beautiful, she said. 'She looks exactly like you. You are so lucky to have her.'

It felt so good to Adele to have someone in her life who truly cared. Around six –o, clock she asked Beatrice whether she would mind if she went for a walk. She had an inexplicable urge to do so.

'Of course not. That's what I'm here for, to give you a little bit of freedom, 'Beatrice instantly replied.

It felt wonderful to be able to walk around Mitcham in the early evening without Josephine. Although Adele loved her daughter, she very rarely got any time to herself. When she did leave the baby with a friend, she always felt anxious and would rush back as soon as possible.

This particular evening was special. She felt as free as a bird. There was something comforting in the air' and she had a strong intuition that her life would eventually get a lot easier and that something she needed to know would be revealed to her. It would be a great importance to the rest of her life. She walked along the road towards Figg's Marsh. Not many people were about, in the distance there was an old man and three teenagers playing football. Adele had not felt so contented for a long time, and could remember being so elated. She said a little prayer and thanked God for bringing Beatrice back into her life.

On her way home she found herself in Love Lane and then in a small road named Taffy's How. The name had seemed so extraordinary to her ever since she first discovered it, and yet somehow it had a familiar ring. She had a good customer who lived there. For some reason something urged her now to investigate the road more carefully than she had done ever before. It was as though her mind was trying to let her know that there was something there that she needed to discover.

Nineteen

She looked at her watch and realised that she had been gone for two and a half- hours and so felt it was her duty to return home.

'Did you have a nice walk?' Beatrice greeted her.

'Yes, all thanks to you.'

'That smells good, what are you making?'

'Dumpling stew. Don't you remember this used to be one of your favourite meals?'

'How could I forget. You didn't have to do the cooking.'

'It's all right, I wanted to.'

'Well, I'm not going to argue with you. How's Josephine?'

'She's been asleep for the last hour and a half. She's such a contented child. I can't get over how much she resembles you.'

Is that a good thing or a bad thing?'

Beatrice realised that Adele was not joking but was asking a straight forward question.

'A good thing of course, you're beautiful and your child is beautiful.'

'I've always been told I look exactly like my uncle.'

'You do. He's a very handsome man. It's his personality that isn't so great, but yours is wholesome and lovely. Adele, and one day you will realise that.'

Adele went into the bedroom to look at Josephine, who was happily sleeping. She indeed was a happy child. Whenever she looked at her baby, she was overjoyed. She stroked her face, and looked at her tiny feet, chuckling silently as she remembered the occasion that her uncle had accused her of giving Josephine bunions because the booties she had bought her were too tight. She thought at the time that there might have been some truth in this, but the doctor had laughed when she told him and she had realised that her uncle had spoken out of ignorance. She took another glimpse at Josephine, and smiled, wondering if she would ever meet the right man, settle down and have another child.

She walked back to the kitchen where Beatrice was stirring the stew. There was an empty plastic bag lying next to the bread bin.

'Shall I throw this out?' Adele asked.

'No, why? Why are you smiling?'

'I've just remembered the time that uncle Marlon put on an old pair of shoes into a plastic bag. And when he realised that he would never wear them again, he threw them away kept the bag. I asked him if I should throw it away, but he said no because he was going to use it for his sandwiches the next day.'

Beatrice also found this funny. It was wonderful for Adele to have somebody around with a sense of humour. It was the sort of company she had missed and needed.

The following day Adele went out for an early evening walk. Once more she proceeded towards Figg's Marsh first. She always felt good for some reason when she saw the tall trees. There was so much uncertainty in her life, and so many doubts about her future. Adele began to feel sometimes that she was entitled to happiness, the trees gave her a feeling of hope and freedom.

In truth, her uncle's behaviour had affected her very badly. It had for one thing made her very wary of men. Although she had a relationship with Simon, she could never have settled down with him for fear he would turn on her as Marlon had done. He had treated her like dirt and made her feel worthless and guilty all the time. If for example, she was having a short nap, he would tell her that there was plenty of housework to be done and that she should not waste her time sleeping during the day. The fact that she might have been up half of the night studying made no difference to him. There was no point in arguing with him because, with his greater experience, he was always able to turn the situation around to make it look as if she was in the wrong, so much so that sometimes she believed it! It was a form indoctrination.

When she saw the trees in Figg's Marsh, they seemed to be telling her that she was free, that she was rid of uncle Marlon and that a new life was ahead of her. For a short time she was able to forget the reality that she was all alone except for her road ahead was uncertain. It was only for a short time she had been deeply hurt and could not easily forget the past. She needed healing, but that was not easy when she recalled her uncle's comments that men would just use her. Her uncle had said it would be hard to find a man to marry her because she had a child at such a young age, which meant that she had a bad reputation. She had disgraced him, he told her, and had brought disgrace to the area they lived in.

She was not too concerned about men for herself. She cherished the hope that eventually her life would improve and that she would find a decent man who would be a good husband and, more importantly, a father for Josephine. Was her uncle right or would she one day fall in love with someone who would want to be with her and Josephine for the rest of there lives? The thought of love occupied her mind, as she crossed Figg's Marsh and looked up at the sky, Adele realised with a sense of shock that she did not really know what love was; she had so little experience of it. Perhaps true love did not exist.

She knew it was now time to go back home but instead of taking the direct route, she found herself walking along Love Lane and then turned right at Taffy's How. This time she went towards the end of the road and noticed a small alleyway, she had never seen before. It was beginning to get dark. She was hesitant about exploring the small path and stood still for a moment as if she was in a dream. There was a powerful scent in the air, a curious mixture of roses, lavender and peppermint. As she looked down the pathway light was shinning brighter than the street lamps. It seemed to tell her that it was there for her protection and she was meant to be there at that precise time, and that it was safe to walk along the path.

All of a sudden, she came across a path of red and white roses on one side and lavender on the other, row after row of them. How come she hadn't noticed it before? The aroma was tremendous, and it felt as though she was in paradise. Nobody else was there but her. It was as though the flowers were there for her personally. She stood rooted to the spot, viewing there beauty and breathing the air. She then moved further down the path, which had now widened, until she came across a peppermint farm. She had never seen a field of peppermints before and there intoxicating scent removed all doubts that had assailed her mind. She experienced perfect peace. She also came across acres of vegetables and glorious flowers- daffodils, narcissi, pinks, cornflowers, sweet peas, and chrysanthemums. She had never encountered such beauty.

In the distance she saw some cottages, sturdily built in brick with slate roofs, unlike any she had ever seen. For some reason she knocked on the third cottage, and a woman answered. Adele had no idea who she was but she was convinced that she had met her before.

'Come in, Adele.'

'I don't know whether I should. After all I don't really know you.' Her deep green eyes captivated her in a loving way.

'Don't worry. It's getting dark outside. Why don't you come in and I'll make you a hot drink?'

The woman obviously knew her, but Adele panicked slightly about finding her way home in the dark. As if reading her mind, the woman said:

'Don't worry, I'll walk back with you to make sure you get back safely.'

Adele was so used to people wrongly thinking they knew how she felt that she was quite astonished by someone who could interpret her thoughts so accurately. She felt reassured and entered the cottage with intrigue.

'Please sit down.'

Inside, the cottage was warm and cosy. There was a rocking chair in the far corner of the front room, which looked as though it was well used, but Adele placed herself on a wooden chair with comfortable cushions. Although the room was small, there was something spacious about it. An indian rug lay on the shiny floor and a coal fire was slowly burning away in the fireplace.

There were many pictures on the wall and in one particular attracted her attention. She could not take her eyes off it. When the woman was in the kitchen making a hot drink, Adele stood up and examined the picture closely. To her amazement, it was a photograph of her late mother. 'Who was this woman, who?

'There you are, Adele.' The woman reappeared, interrupting her thoughts. Her voice was soft and gentle. 'I'm sorry, I've run out of hot chocolate, so I've made you some peppermint tea. I hope you don't mind.'

'No, that's fine.'

'Let me introduce myself to you,' the woman said. 'My name is Mrs How – Taffy How.'

'But that's the name of the little road around the corner, Taffy's how. It's very unusual.'

'Yes I know, but that's my name.'

The fresh smell of peppermint relaxed Adele and for the first time she had a good look at the woman. Peace and joy seemed to emanate from her. Her dark brown eyes stood out, seemingly filled with love and understanding. Her face was quite beautiful. She had brown hair and an olive complexion. It was impossible to say how old she was. She was not young but she was not what Adele thought of as an old woman.

It felt weird being in her presence, but not in a frightening or unpleasant way. Adele had the impression Taffy had travelled a long way to get there, and from another world, but she was living in Mitcham!

It was all very mystifying and dreamlike. Finally Adele plucked up courage to ask;

'Can I ask you how you knew my mum?'

'Yes, of course you can. I'm sure you must have seen the picture of your mother.

'Yes.'

'Well, I knew your mum.'

'But how?'

'It goes back a few centuries. Our ancestors knew each other well. In those days families were very close and helped each other much more.'

'What do you mean?'

'People had much more time for each other. Families listened more, and were there to help resolve their problems. Relatives looked after children. If they needed financial help, they were there for you. If you needed a roof over your head, they would make sure that your needs were met. There was just so much love and togetherness. In those days families were real families.'

Adele listened with growing interest to what Taffy was saying. She could not deny that modern society was less compassionate. She did not want to criticise all families, but her own experience with her uncle and her grandparents had shown her how unhelpful and even uncaring families could be.

'I'm not saying that everything was better in the past,' Taffy continued, 'because today you can get so much help from the government or the council. I believe that the families aren't as close as they used to be. You found that out for yourself.

Again Taffy seemed to be reading Adele's thoughts.

'Your mother also needed help,' she went on, 'in the same way as you do now I helped her, and I promised her I would help you. I arranged that we should meet.'

'How' Adele asked?'

'Something drew you to me. That's all you need to know. You will not always be able to find me, I hope I will always be here for you, I hope. What I want to tell you is the best help is the help you give yourself. You can develop a sense of positive power, which will enlighten your life, particularly if you have faith in God.'

'How can I do this?

One way is to get rid of all fear and all negative attitudes to life. Your mother knew that many women destroy their lives through negative thinking. She became angry about certain things in her own life. Anger is not a bad thing if it is used in the right way. It creates energy if you let it work for you, rather than against you. An inner energy can help you do those things that need doing.

'What do you mean?' Adele asked. She was able to follow the drift of Taffy's advice but at times the woman seemed to be talking in riddles.

'For instance, when your uncle criticised you...'

'How did you know?' Adele asked.

'I've been watching you but I can't explain. Just trust me. When uncle Marlon called you a parasite, you could have answered him back and sought revenge. Naturally angry it was probably better to harness your anger and let it work for you in order to help you progress in your everyday life.'

'I'm not sure I understand.'

'Let me give you an example. Say that your house needs cleaning but you haven't got the energy, or you just can't be bothered to clean it. You could turn your anger into energy, using it to clean the house. In your case if you feel angry you could work harder, giving yourself the added energy to drop more catalogues and pick up more orders. There are so many different things you can do to create a better life for yourself if you think positively instead of allowing negative attitudes to hold you back.'

Adele Wondered how Taffy knew about her part-time work. Then Taffy gave her an example of a swimmer who had developed a positive way of thinking.

'She was just an ordinary person like you and me and she was having all sorts of problems in her life. Many people had hurt her, and I told her exactly what I'm telling you. She said she would put my ideas into practice.'

'How did she do that?'

'Swimming was her only form of exercise, and she used it positively to release her anger. She found that her speeds were improving rapidly, and began to stand out, so much so that she was invited to join a swimming team. This was her dream come true and continued to use this positive approach until she was asked if she would like to train for the Olympics.

It was only when she was lining up for the first serious race that her doubts returned and her mind relapsed into all the old negative thoughts that she had put behind her. Adele became hesitant and told herself that she couldn't compete at the top level. Something was holding her back. In fact when the whistle blew and the race started, it was all she could do to jump into the water. It felt as though hands were pulling her down, wanting her to go under and drown. In a flash, she remembered the positive messages I had taught her, and the anger she now felt for her stupidity propelled her forward. She had some leeway to make up but she decided then and there that she was going to win if she possibly could. And would you believe she did? She told me later that she thought about the verbal abuse she had received from a boyfriend, and this triggered her reaction.'

Adele was not sure she could believe this story. Was it really possible to achieve so much just by thinking positively? She so much wanted to tell Taffy about her own life, but the woman seemed to know all about her. As if reading her thoughts, Taffy said:

I also know you've been hurt very badly, perhaps even more than you realise. I know that if you don't sort yourself out now, you could destroy your life and even your daughter's. You need help. A young girl like you can't do everything on her own. Your mother knew what I told you but she didn't believe it could work, and because she left it too late and refused to discuss how she was feeling or even to acknowledge that there was anything wrong, she did not even get the help that she needed. You know your mum died of liver disease, partly due to drinking too much she was depressed. That's why I want to help you and answer some of the questions that are on your mind.

Twenty

Adele opened her heart to Taffy, starting with her relationship with her uncle and culminating in the birth of little Josephine. Taffy seemed to know without being told but it helped Adele to confide in somebody, especially somebody as wise and kind as this strange woman, whose great compassion was evident in her voice and whose words were soothing and healing.

Taffy explained that Uncle Marlon's resentment might have arisen from the fact that he would have preferred to bring up his own daughter rather than his niece.

'Try to forgive him,' she advised. 'I know it's not easy but it is important in life to turn your bad experiences to advantage. If you are able to forgive, or at least understand, you will yourself grow into a better person by learning from the situation, and will come out mentally stronger so that you are able to deal with whatever arises in the future ,much better. If you can find it in your heart to forgive your uncle, you will get rid of all the pain you are suffering, it will make you a better person. You will be amazed at how you will start enjoying your life again. It's important to deal with the way that you feel, then put it behind you and get on with your life.'

'If I forgive Uncle Marlon, how will I be able to use my anger, as you advised me?'

'That's a very astute question for such a young lady,' Taffy complimented her. 'Yes, if you are angry, it is a good thing to use it constructively, but it is better still if you can get rid of it. Whether you have managed it once and for all, or whether it lingers in you, you must face all challenges in life with positive energy, and will be surprised at what you can achieve. Then you will find that you feel content, and eventually even the anger you have for your uncle will disappear.'

Adele was so absorbed in what Taffy was saying that she completely lost all sense of time and place. She seemed to be in the real world but at the same time she seemed to be part of a dream. Perhaps she even fell asleep, because she suddenly awoke into a state of awareness and called out:

'what time is it?'

'It's two o'clock.'

'Yes, two o'clock in the morning' said Taffy

'How could time have flown by like that?'

'I was going to take you home but it's too late now'. Taffy said. 'What you can do is sleep here on the sofa. I'll get you a blanket and then you can leave first thing in the morning.'

What about Josephine and Beatrice?' Adele was suddenly alarmed that she had left them for too long.

'Don't worry, they'll be fine.' There was an authority in Taffy's voice that reassured Adele. 'They won't be worried about you.'

Adele slept well she woke up at six o' clock and left a note for Taffy, thanking her for her hospitality, she peered down at her whilst she slept her eyes flickered, as if she knew Adele was watching her. Her jet black hair lay on the pillow like it had just been brushed into that position. She looked so beautiful as she admired her rosy cheeks. She reminded her of her daughter - the same peace.

Adele felt as though she was stepping out into the countryside as she left Taffy's cottage. The air was fresh and the beautiful flowers seemed to welcome her. She had never felt so emotionally safe, as she set out on her short walk home with a feeling of tremendous hope. Deep within she knew that changes were going to take place in her life, as she had now made the decision to forgive her uncle, and even to love him. By expelling a whole lot of turmoil from her mind, she would create room to start thinking positively about her life and of course about Josephine's future

She did not remember about actually discussing men with Taffy but now she could hear the wise woman's words in her head. Taffy had told her, or was telling her, that not all men were the same. Provided she was careful about whom she dated and sought advice from people who lived decent lives, she would one day meet someone who would make an ideal husband for her and father for Josephine. It felt good to be able to think so positively about the future.

When she arrived home, Beatrice and Josephine were still fast asleep.

Adele's life did improve and she continued to keep in contact with Beatrice. She forgave her uncle and visited him from time to time, and because she was know living away from home with her daughter, he slowly began to respect her and they developed a better relationship.

She tried looking for Taffy a few days after the visit but could not locate her or her home. It was as if the area and even the alleyway did not exist. She was convinced however that Taffy had moved on because there were other people in desperate need of her help. The thought that Taffy was no longer there did not sadden Adele because she was grateful that she had spoken to her, and whenever she observed the natural beauty of life, Taffy came into her mind. It reminded her to think positively and to be grateful that she was privileged to be alive in a world which despite its problems and horrors, held infinite love and a cascade of beauty.